Sherlock Holmes
Travels in the Canadian West

The great spaces above …

Sherlock Holmes

Travels in the Canadian West

from the annals of
John H. Watson, M.D.

Ronald C. Weyman

Simon & Pierre
Toronto, Canada

Illustrations: American Museum of Natural History: 103; British Columbia Archives and Records Service: cover, 95, 118, 123, 127; Edward R. Curtis, Northern Vancouver Island, B.C., 1914: 107; Glenbow Archives, Calgary, Alberta: frontispiece; Glenbow Foundation, lithographs by George Catlin: 68, 71; Glenbow Photograph, Calgary, Alberta, engraving by Frederic S. Remington: 28; Anna Harriette Leonowens Collection: 99; National Archives of Canada: 8; Photo Nadar, Collection Yvan Christ, Paris: 81.

Editor: Jean Paton
Designer: Ron & Ron Design and Photography
Printed and bound in Canada

The writing of this manuscript and the publication of this book were made possible by support from several sources. We would like to acknowledge the generous assistance and ongoing support of **The Canada Council, The Book Publishing Industry Development Program** of the **Department of Canadian Heritage, The Ontario Arts Council,** and **The Ontario Publishing Centre** of the **Ministry of Culture, Tourism and Recreation.**

J. Kirk Howard, President

1 2 3 4 5 . 9 8 7 6 5

Canadian Cataloguing in Publication Data

Weyman, Ronald C., 1915-
    Sherlock Holmes : travels in the Canadian West

ISBN 0-88924-245-3

I. Title.

PS8595.E96S58 1994   C813'.54   C94-932199-0
PR9199.3.W48S58 1994

Order from Simon & Pierre Publishing Co. Ltd., care of

Dundurn Press Limited	Dundurn Distribution	Dundurn Press Limited
2181 Queen Street East	73 Lime Walk	1823 Maryland Avenue
Suite 301	Headington, Oxford	P.O. Box 1000
Toronto, Canada	England	Niagara Falls, N.Y.
M4E 1E5	0X3 7AD	U.S.A. 14302-1000

Contents

Illustrations

Foreword

In all my adventures with my dear friend Sherlock Holmes, rarely was I called upon to go far beyond the limits of the city of London, whereas he from time to time would disappear on urgent missions to the capitals of Europe and the Near East, from Paris to Istanbul; excursions from which I would be excluded, may I say, with some regret, and indeed envy. Returning from such exotic locations, he would make the most casual and tantalizing references to his mission, frequently leaving me at a loss what to set down for the record.

Ironically, here in Canada, where I am now in company with Holmes, I am prohibited from presenting for publication any of the voluminous notes I have been taking, because in the eyes of the world Holmes is officially deceased, having been swept over the notorious Reichenbach Falls in Switzerland, and his body not recovered.

That this "death" of Holmes, mourned by so many, was in fact a ploy of the British Foreign office to allow Holmes to go underground initially on matters of the gravest importance to Britain, is a secret which perhaps will never be revealed.

For the record, however, I feel that I must make notes of what really happened in those adventurous years, as far as I am able, before Holmes' return to life is officially approved.

From notes by Doctor Watson
dated 1892
Beaver Valley, Ontario

… our guide, a Métis …

1

Sherlock Holmes and the Wendigo

Sherlock Holmes peered intently at the mark in the snow. It was the size of a large human footprint, or perhaps that of a bear. It had been made recently, because the edges of the mark were quite sharp. The print was more deeply impressed at one end than the other, where a scattering of snow had been thrown in a forward direction.

"It moves to the north," said Holmes. "Into the Barren Lands."

He peered ahead, and our guide muttered to himself.

"The Indian fellow doesn't seem too happy," I observed.

"He has little reason to be," replied Holmes. "He believes it to be the mark of the Wendigo." Holmes moved abruptly, following the direction in which the mysterious print pointed.

"Here is another one, Watson," cried Holmes.

"It must be fully six feet away from the first," I said, catching up to him.

"That is an impossible human stride. The Indians believe it to be super-human, and they are fearful of it." Holmes was already moving ahead, in line with the two mysterious marks. "And a third imprint," he cried in a moment. "Fully twenty feet away."

He pressed on, his keen eyes examining the surface of the snow. A gentle wind was blowing from the south, a rare thing in those northern Canadian parts at that time of year, sifting the light snow covering. It was early in the winter season.

Presently came a hail from Holmes. "Over here, Watson. Yet another mark." He was on his knees in the snow, quizzing glass to his eye, when I caught up. "A full fifty feet from the last," he said. "Not so markedly indented. As if ..." He looked up at the sky, which had become overcast. The thin wind was blowing snow, and the mysterious indentation was already losing its shape and definition, as if the agent, human or otherwise, had been lifted into the sky.

The wind gusted at that moment, and borne upon it, from the great spaces above us, came a forlorn note like that of a lost soul.

"Sky ... Wendigo ..." said our guide. He pointed upwards.

In my limited contact with North American natives to date, I had seen no evidence of fear. I had seen anger, stolidity and laughter, but this fellow was demonstrating an emotion I had not experienced before. The setting, I realized, was quite unique. Elsewhere in the world, for example in India where I had served with the Indian Army, no matter where one was, there was always evidence of mankind, sometimes dating back thousands of years. In the middle of a desert or jungle one would come upon ancient carvings or tombs, the remains of vast cities, relics which bore mute testimony to the glories of past civilizations.

In the Canadian north, there was no such context. Man has never put his mark on the rugged landscape since the beginning of time. The natives of this country have lived here for a thousand years or more, revering the land, the forest, and their fellow inhabitants — the bear and the moose, the eagle, the bison and the rattlesnake. Each has its place in the scheme of things. But to the stranger newly arrived from a European culture, much of this raw contact with nature, and the lack of physical evidence of the presence and the superiority of man, was disturbing.

And so it was on this occasion. A few mysterious marks in the snow, the evocation of strange and powerful forces in the wilderness. I found myself shivering under my heavy fur parka.

Holmes glanced up at the sky. "The wind, at the moment, is from the south, is it not, Watson?"

"Yes, it is, Holmes."

"And the direction of those mysterious indentations in the snow?"

"To the north."

"As a sea-faring man, what does that suggest to you?"

"That whatever agent caused the marks in the snow was influenced by the direction of the wind."

"Excellent, Watson." Holmes banged his gloved hands together. "There is little more we can do now, so I suggest we return to the camp and have a cup of hot tea."

My friend spoke to our Indian companion with a word or two of Ojibway. It never ceases to amaze me the manner in which Holmes is able to assume the identity and coloration of wherever he happens to be. Our guide nodded, and turning, led the way back to the sparse line of trees.

As we approached the encampment from whence we had started earlier in the day, there was a sound of Indian drums, and the wail of song from half a dozen throats. I have been told that the North American Indian has songs for every imaginable occasion, from celebration of the birth of a new child to the death-song of a brave, but for the life of me I could detect but little difference in the musical substance and inflection from one to another.

The sound of the drums grew louder, and as we approached, dogs from the camp came out to investigate our presence, sniffing at our heels until our brave dismissed them with a well-placed kick or two. The acrid smell of wood smoke hung in the air, and the odour of roasting venison. I realized that I was hungry after a day on the trail.

Our guide, a Métis fellow by the name of Pelletier, came towards us from the camp.

"How is our patient?" I asked him.

"Still in a coma," he replied. "De warriors are 'aving a ritual to drive out de evil spirit."

"The Wendigo," said Holmes.

"Exactement, m'sieur."

"But the Wendigo has gone."

"It will come back, m'sieur, to claim its victim. It always 'appen."

"The Wendigo," said Holmes. "What is it?"

"Diet," I said.

"M'sieur?" Pelletier had turned towards me.

"The things you eat. Venison, cranberry. Roots you dig out of the ground."

"Wit' respect, m'sieur, the Indians 'ave been living 'ere for a t'ousand years, an' do not need h'instruction on what to h'eat from de newcomer w'ite man. Dere are times, of course, w'en de 'unting is bad, an' people could go crazy starving. But dat does not h'explain footprints in de snow h'as if someone 'ad jumped into de sky." He made a broad gesture with his arm at the vastness above our heads.

We reached the encampment. Dog sleds were up-ended as windbreaks. Indian teepees were dug into the snow, great sheets of birchbark providing insulation. Across a blazing log fire, a quarter of venison was roasting, spitting its melting fat into the flames. From inside the largest teepee came the beat of drums, setting one's nerves on edge, as the vibrations called up some atavistic response from deep within one's nature.

"May we enter, Henri, do you think?" said Holmes.

"You are 'ere as medicine man, M'sieur 'olmes. You do as you wish."

It was surprisingly warm inside the teepee. A small, bright fire burned in the centre, its smoke cunningly directed through a vent in the peak, which I observed was controlled by two cedar poles, adjusting the aperture to the direction of the wind, and thus creating a draft.

Two natives banged with sticks upon drums, hides of some sort stretched tightly over wooden hoops, making the throbbing rhythm that had aroused me as we approached the camp. Inside the teepee, the sound was overwhelming. I had the feeling of being hauled back into the past, untouched by civilization. On the far side of the fire, a wolf-like creature was crouched over the naked figure of a young warrior, lying unconscious on a bear skin. With sweeping gestures, the wolf appeared to be clawing at the prone figure, which gleamed wet with perspiration in the flickering light from the fire. As it clawed, the creature left trails of black and vermilion on the brown body.

"Some kind of exorcism," observed Holmes.

"It would appear to be," I replied.

At the sound of our voices, the wolf-like creature turned towards us with a snarl, its upraised claws dripping with what appeared to be blood. I was quite shocked with the savage power that was momentarily focussed upon me. Dark eyes bore into mine. Open jaws disclosed the glistening canines of a giant wolf, reaching, I felt, for my throat. Then I realized that the glowing eyes were fixed in a hallucinatory manner. The jaws, though real enough, were part of the head-dress of the medicine man, who had assumed this guise to pursue his goal —

the exorcism of the spirit that presumably had the young warrior under its thrall.

The intensity of the drums increased. The great wolf made a sweeping gesture over the fire, which at once glittered with a thousand points of light. From the flames arose a cloud of incense, and I had a momentary vision of a priestly acolyte in St. Paul's Cathedral, that centre of Christendom, swinging his aromatic censer in front of the High Altar, and chanting the Creed.

The wolf growled some savage formula into the flames, and threw on another handful of the pungent incense. The drums reached a crescendo. My senses were being swayed by their power, and by the aromatic smoke. I felt that I might be caught up in hallucinatory delusions.

I shifted my gaze to Holmes. He sat there, cross-legged in this primitive place, his aquiline features lit by the flames from the fire, and I felt curiously cut off from my old friend. It was as if he were one with this ancient ritual of savage sorcery, while I was alone with the tattered remnants of European culture.

I tried to shrug off this feeling, and turned my attention to the patient, who until now had been lying naked and rigid on the bearskin on the floor of the teepee. Through the smoke I could see his brown body streaming, as if lacerated with the vermilion and black mixture that the wolf-mystic had applied. The face in particular looked gruesome, painted in a fashion that gave a lopsided leer to the visage as if he enjoyed a private and macabre joke.

As I watched, the drumming stopped abruptly, and in the silence one could hear the heavy breathing of the drummers and the rustle of the flames in the fire. The medicine man was silent beside the burning embers. Then he lifted his head and gave a long wolf-like wail that raised the hair on the back of my neck. He paused. From the woods outside came a response: from the lone wastes of the snow-bound wilderness came a chorus of wolf-howls that in some curious way was reassuring to me. It touched some inner chord in my being.

Our medicine man howled again, this time with a different inflection, followed by a series of short intimate yelps. The distant chorus replied in kind, and as I peered through the clearing smoke from the fire towards the patient, I saw his rigid muscles relax, and presently his eyes opened. A few moments later he sat up and looked around, his eyes bright with calm intelligence.

The drummers grunted, and laying aside their drums, pulled on caribou parkas before going out of the teepee. The medicine man followed, ignoring us completely. Then our guide, Henri, entered the teepee with a steaming can of hot tea. He took it first to the young warrior who sat there on the bearskin, pulling a robe about himself. The latter grunted his thanks, and took a long pull at the hot liquid before passing it to Holmes.

"Jolly good," said Holmes.

My turn was next. The tea was strong, sweetened with maple sap. I drank with pleasure, then passed it to Henri.

"May I examine the patient, Henri?" I asked.

"Oui, m'sieur. But of course. The Wendigo 'as gone, the patient is better."

I conducted the usual tests, heart, lungs, eyes, co-ordination. "A normal, healthy, intelligent young man, Holmes. In the prime of life."

"Yet this is the same fellow that had to be physically restrained for fear he would murder his wife and children."

"Oui, m'sieur. It 'as 'appen before. The power of the Wendigo."

"What would you say, Watson?"

"Tropical diseases are my forte, Holmes, not self-induced paranoia."

"Paranoia?"

"A fellow in Berlin has come up with the theory that much aberrant human conduct, and indeed physical sickness, can be induced by one's own mental processes. In India I witnessed a perfectly healthy man, told by a fakir that his time was up, simply stop living."

"But in this case, Watson?" Holmes' voice was crisp.

"You saw the amazing powers of the medicine man, Holmes. If he chose to turn them to evil purposes...." I left the sentence unfinished.

Our young patient had pulled on some clothing, and now, ignoring us, he went outside.

"How does the action of the medicine man relate to the Wendigo?" Holmes turned to Henri, who was filling a blackened clay pipe with tobacco. "Henri?"

"To me, m'sieur, it is a mystery."

Holmes had taken out his own worn briar pipe, and Pelletier smiled as he saw it. He passed over the leather pouch.

"Tabac — habitant, m'sieur."

"Merci, Henri," replied Holmes, and taking the sack filled his pipe and in a moment was puffing away happily. "If there is more tea, I could do with another cup," he said.

"Moment, m'sieur." Our guide stuck his head out of the tent flap, and said something to an unseen person outside in the lilting Ojibway tongue. He was answered by a saucy female voice, and when he withdrew his head, he was smiling.

"Some of dose femmes are h'embarrassing, messieurs. Dat one dere 'as h'eyes on your Doctor Watson."

"On me?" I said.

"Dat w'at she say. She like your mustache." I stroked my mustache, thinking it was somewhat overgrown these days, so far from a civilized barber, but such is my nature that I involuntarily warmed to the compliment passed on from the unseen female.

"How old is the Wendigo story, Henri?" asked Holmes presently.

"Since before my time, m'sieur."

"Did it always make marks in the snow?"

"Not always, m'sieur. But there was always a time w'en a fellow would go mad and follow de Wendigo into de woods, or into de Barren Lands. Sometimes 'e would return an' commit murder, cutting off de 'eads an' h'eating de flesh of 'is h'own family. I ..." He broke off at this point as the tent flaps were pushed open and a slender Indian maid thrust her way in, her black shining hair swinging to her waist. She shoved a can of hot tea into Pierre's hands, with some comment in her lilting language, and turned on her moccasined heel towards the exit. As she did so, she smiled at me through the cascade of dark hair. I could not resist a smile of approval at the beauty of her appearance and her movement.

"So the marks made in the snow by this most recent appearance are unusual, are they?" went on Holmes, ignoring the interruption, but grateful for his share of the hot, sweet tea.

"Unusual, m'sieur? De Wendigo come an' go, 'owever it want. Not'ing is ever usual, m'sieur. De fellow dat was 'ere ... "

"The sick man?"

"Early dis morning, dat fellow was frothing at 'is mouth, 'is eyes were wild, and 'e was running off into de Barren Lands h'after de Wendigo."

"Did anyone *see* the Wendigo?"

"No one *sees* it, m'sieur. Or if dey do, dey h'are mad, an' cannot tell about it."

"How did the fellow come back?"

"De braves of de tribe. Dey grab 'im an' pull 'im back. De medicine man does medicine. You see dat yourself."

"And this restored the young man to sanity?"

"Oui m'sieur. Until nex' time."

I noticed that the fire had been smoking for some minutes, causing my eyes to stream. At that moment, the tent began to shake violently, and I thought that some further "medicine" was at work, having heard somewhere of Indian tents shaking without human agency, but no: two fat squaws pushed their way in, and with expertise born of long practice, with the assistance of unseen hands outside, they loosened the fabric of the tent to adjust it some ninety degrees from its previous position. Paying no attention to us, they shifted the tents and the overhead vents to a new position. The fire drew again, and the smoke was drawn up through the vent.

"What was all that about?" I asked, when the women had gone.

"The wind 'as change —" said Pierre, as if that explained everything. "It swing' to the nort'."

"Then perhaps the Wendigo will pass this way again," said Sherlock Holmes. He puffed on his pipe, his eyes glinting in the firelight.

We had dined well on roast venison and ground roots, washed down with tea. I had heard much about the coarse diet of the aboriginals of this country, and indeed, compared with the delicacies of London and Paris, their food was very basic. And yet in a few weeks of adjustment, and with a healthy hunger developed from long days in the outdoors (I had even learned how to paddle a canoe and run with a dog-sled) the scent of venison grilling over an open fire of balsam wood aroused an appetite and an appreciation I had never experienced in the most elegant of European restaurants.

Further, I discovered that the women were most attentive to one's needs, and that within this community of natives there was a kind of sophistication that I never would have suspected. Our medicine man, for instance, having shed his wolfskin guise, proved to be a conjurer of considerable skill, making things vanish and reappear under one's very nose. He did this with a rude patter of jokes, which had the rest of the natives, especially the females, rolling with laughter. I am sure that some of his references had sexual connotations and were directed at Holmes and myself. I found that my mustaches were caressed more than once by the ladies, while my dear Holmes, clean-shaven as he was, and perhaps a little more straight-laced than I, was treated more circumspectly. In any event, the evening passed with considerable merriment, until at last in the glow and warmth of the firelight, Holmes and I tumbled into our sleeping bags, while the Indians found their nests within the teepees and the bearskins of the tiny community.

Beyond the glow of the firelight, the limitless sky above was festooned with the array of stars that over the years I have learned to identify. Sailing into southern waters in the old *Fastnet* and rounding Cape Horn, I had become acquainted with the Southern Cross, and here in the cold northern woods the constellations swung around Polaris, the single stable star in the firmament. In my polar sleeping bag, I fell into dreamless slumber.

When I awakened, the fire had burned low, the constellations had swung above my head, and someone was in the process of joining me. Against the starry sky was the outline of a female form; swiftly, warmly, a nubile figure was in beside me. There was a scent of balsam and of mint, and aromas that touched the centre of my being. There was long dark hair that enveloped me, the warmth of soft lips on my mustache, and supple limbs that entwined me. For a moment I glanced in the direction where I knew Holmes to be sleeping, then I gave myself up to the wave of primitive delight that was offered me.

Morning came. My companion of the night had vanished. The occupants of the camp were already up and about. The squaws had split whitefish from head to tail, and spread them out like Japanese fans on a lattice-work of green sticks, grilling in the heat of the newly invigorated fire. A tin of water boiled on the coals, ready for the inevitable cup of tea.

I looked over in the direction that Holmes had been sleeping. He was no longer there. I had no sooner raised myself on my elbow than his familiar voice accosted me.

"Watson, dear chap. I trust you slept well." I turned my head, and there was Holmes, standing over me, muffled up in furs against the cold.

"Yes, I did, actually, Holmes. Thank you."

"Splendid. Perhaps you would like to join us. Before breakfast."

Behind him was Pelletier and three or four male members of the band. They appeared to be dressed for the trail.

"What's up?" I glanced from one to the other. They waited expectantly.

"Something you would like to see, I'm sure." In my spacious sleeping bag were my trowsers, heavy shirt and parka. In a moment I had pulled them on, and thus equipped joined the group. Wordlessly, they turned away into the fringe of trees that bordered our camp, and beyond into the beginning of the Barrens. I followed in their footsteps.

The wind was now in the north, and came keening across the open spaces with a knife-like edge that attacked the very centre of one's being. Gone was the warmth and comfort of the Indian encampment, however primitive. Here, I felt reduced to insignificance in the face of the unknown.

I noticed that presently the Indian members of our band dropped behind, so that the party became led by Holmes, Pelletier and myself.

"Holmes," I shouted against the frigid wind. I had the hood of my fur parka around my face.

"What?" he cried.

"Why are the Indians dropping back?"

"The Wendigo," he shouted in reply. His words were snatched away by the tempest.

Our trail led to a dip in the land, where a few stunted pine trees eked out a meagre existence. As we came over the rise a curious sound assailed my ears, a flapping sound, as if giant wings were entrapped in the branches of the trees, vainly seeking escape. I raised my head against the northern blast, and saw before me, partly deflated, the rounded surface of a balloon, its loose fabric rippling in the wind. Attached to it was a basket, and in the basket, as we drew closer, horror of horrors! Three men, white of skin, dressed in furs for the northern clime, sprawled in abandoned attitudes, frozen to death!

"Here is your Wendigo," said Holmes.

In a moment he was exploring the basket for evidence of the occupants' purpose. I, my Hippocratic Oath uppermost, checked each of the figures for a sign of life. There was none.

Holmes had found papers and scientific instruments. Attached to a length of coiled cable, a polished tubular steel instrument reflected the sombre light of the day.

"A magnetometer," said Holmes.

"A what, Holmes?" I said.

"An instrument which can detect bodies of ore in the rock," said Holmes. "Modern surveying companies use it to conduct magnetic tests on areas of the earth's surface they think may be worth mining." He brushed the snow off the notebooks. "Judging from these records, their efforts have been rewarded. This appears to be one of the richest deposits of iron ore in the world."

"The Wendigo," said Pelletier.

"What's that you say?"

"De creature of de Nort' dat lures man to madness and death."

Holmes lowered his head in tribute to the ironic truth of Pelletier's statement.

"I should have known yesterday," said Holmes.

"How could you know?"

"The marks in the snow. It was an unseasonably south wind, Watson. You noted that."

"Yes."

"The marks were made by the magnetometer dangling from the balloon until it had gained sufficient altitude to operate efficiently."

It was beginning to snow, and through the murk came the throb of an Indian drum, and the chant of a death song.

"When the wind finally changed, the balloon was blown back again. The sharp drop in temperature did the rest. Those unfortunate fellows. Where were they from, do you suppose?"

"Some international mining consortium, judging from their notes."

We turned from the forlorn wreckage of this demonstration of modern aeronautical science. Holmes retained the magnetometer, the notebooks and personal papers, to forward to the appropriate authorities. As we returned to the camp, we were followed by the Indians moving slowly to the beat of their drum.

When we reached camp, the young Indian brave, Eagle Rib, my recent patient, was not to be seen. Alone, he had walked away from his community into the stark lonely mystery of the Barren Lands. The wind increased, and from far away I heard the sound of a wolf crying in wilderness. Or perhaps it was the cry of the Wendigo.

2

The Mystery of
Headless Valley

CHAPTER ONE

The Lady in the Bath

I have always found it curious that whereas the manner of life in Britain's upper classes in the time of our revered Queen Victoria is frequently quite licentious, so little reflection of this appears in the accepted literature of the time.

It is well-known, for instance, that our own beloved "Bertie," Prince of Wales, heir to the throne, is a profligate of considerable practice, and his mother has been at her wits' end finding an acceptable bride for him. The average man on the street accepts these peccadilloes as a matter of course, and if anything, sees them as an acceptable standard of royal conduct. This is not to cast any aspersions on the habits of Her Gracious Majesty and her consort Prince Albert. Perhaps it is indeed their propriety that has been instrumental in pushing Bertie into his sometimes questionable behaviour.

In any event, a number of the cases in which I have collaborated with my dear friend Sherlock Holmes, have had as their focus peccadilloes not uncommon to the time, but I have been obliged to couch these affairs in such ambiguous terms as to render them virtually pointless, and in fact, to refrain from publishing them at all.

It is only by accident, I am sure, that Holmes and his publishers let my reference to my own experience with women extending over many nations and on three separate continents, slip through, this being one specific and truthful measure of the time.

These thoughts occurred to me while in the town of Calgary in the winter of 1892, seeking one Reggie Braithwaite, the wayward son of an old fellow-medical student of mine at Bart's. The young man had seemingly emigrated to Canada, and had joined the North West Mounted Police, somewhere in that great country's Western frontier region.

Arriving at the railway station, I was given the address of what I was led to believe was the town's best hotel. A cabby took me there, and deposited me and my baggage at the door with a cheerful enough demeanour, and the words, "They'll look after you here, sorr. All the comforts of home."

"Thank you, my man," I said, and tipped the fellow liberally for his assistance. He clucked to his horse, and drove away.

I stood on the snowy steps of the relatively imposing building, I say "relatively," for the further I went west in this country, the newer and sparser the settlements became, and I longed at times for the familiar architecture of dear old London. For a new frontier experience, however, this was pleasant enough: the glow of light from within as the daylight faded; the scent of wood smoke on the cold air; the sound of a piano playing a familiar music hall ballad.

I pushed open the door to find myself in a pleasant reception room. It was warm and welcoming, a wood fire burning in the fireplace. There was a scattering of easy chairs and tables at which sat groups of men and young women taking their ease playing cards, reading, or engaged in merry conversation. At the piano sat a lady of imposing appearance and cheerful countenance. Beside her, singing quite melodiously, was a young man I judged to be a cowboy from his garb, Stetson hat pushed back on his head. Another fellow stood beside the piano, attempting to scrape a tune out of a fiddle. The lady looked up at my entrance, and with a flourish, finished the piece she was playing. She got up and came towards me.

"Welcome, sir," she said.

"Madam," I said. "Are you the proprietress?"

"Indeed I am," she replied. "Polly Perkins is the name." Her face was skillfully made up, her figure well-proportioned in a fashionable dress.

"Do you have a room, Miss Perkins?" I enquired. "I am just off the train. John Watson is the name."

"English," she said smiling.

"Yes, your hotel was recommended to me."

"In England? Surely not."

"No. By the good fellow that drove me here from the station."

"Of course," she said warmly. "I'll have one of the girls show you the room. Would you like a good hot tub first?"

"Madam," I said, "that would be more than welcome."

"I have just had modern plumbing installed. The water is hot, and I shall have it run for you." She turned from me for a moment. "Colette," she called.

At one of the tables, a young lady turned her head towards us. "Madame?"

"Come here a moment, would you?"

The girl excused herself from the table, and came towards us. I was conscious of black hair, dark eyes, and a fetching décolleté.

"This is Colette," said Polly Perkins. "Colette, this is Mr. Watson."

"Doctor, actually," said I.

"Doctor Watson wishes a bath, Colette. Would you see to it?"

"Right away, madam." The girl gave me a demure smile, and turned towards the stair. "Bring your bag, Doctor Watson," she cried.

I humped my bag up the stairs, conscious of Colette's feminine presence ahead of me. On the landing she opened a door.

"You can make yourself comfortable in your room while your bath is being drawn. I'll send up some champagne."

"What?" I cried. "Champagne?"

"Courtesy of the establishment, sir," she gave me a smile and was gone, closing the door gently behind her.

"Well," I thought as I sat down on the bed to take off my boots, "This is a bit of all right."

I had opened my bag and taken out my dressing-gown, slippers, and shaving kit, and there came a tap on the door.

"Come," I cried, struggling into my dressing gown. The door opened and a pert little negro lass entered, carrying a tray upon which was balanced a bottle of French champagne, two glasses and some English water biscuits. The girl smiled at me shyly and placed the tray on the side-table. She had left the door open, and my eye was drawn to the corridor, where two figures were coming out of a nearby room.

One was a tall, lean cowboy figure who, walking with that singular legs-apart gait one sees in the West, clapped a battered black Stetson hat upon his head, and smiled in a satisfied manner as his arm went around his companion, a pert little red headed lady. They looked like honeymooners, although I began to feel a little doubtful.

The little negress had barely departed when Colette re-appeared, breezing into the room with an uncommon air of intimacy, I thought.

"Ah, good," she said. "The champagne." And without further ado, with considerable expertise, she had the cork popped out of the bottle, and was pouring the beverage, sparkling and fizzing, into the two glasses.

"What's your first name?" she said, while thus engaged.

"John," I said.

"Well, John," she said, handing me a glass, and keeping one for herself. "Nice to make your acquaintance. Bottoms up." So saying, she clinked glasses, and gulped the contents of hers in a draught. "I'll just go and check on your bath, John. The bathroom's at the end of the hall. Bring the bottle when you're ready. We can finish it in the tub." With which parting observation she left me to my thoughts.

I had grown used to the free and easy manners of many of the people I had met in Canada, and the way in which a stranger, casually met in a train or on a boat, would often plunge at once into intimate details of his own life, and expect one's reciprocation as a matter of course. But to check into an hotel on the Canadian prairies, and have a complimentary bottle of French champagne shared in one's bedroom by an attractive young person of the opposite sex, was, I must admit, outside my experience until now.

I finished the contents of my own glass with considerable pleasure, however, and re-filled it. I found a turkish towel hanging on the back of the door, and in slippers and dressing gown, turkish towel around my neck, the champagne bottle and glass in my hands, I made my way down the hall, to where I could hear water running and see steam escaping from a doorway.

I entered, and found myself in a small room. Through the mist, I could see a great cast-iron bathtub, half-full of hot soapy water. The suds and the mist, between them, helped to conceal in part the delightful figure of Colette. She was already in the bath, quite naked. I gazed at her in astonishment. She laughed at me gaily, and held out her champagne glass.

"Come on in, John," she cried. "Get in and I'll scrub your back!"

It was only then that I realized the true character of the establishment to which I had come, and such is my nature, that after a brief moment of hesitation, I flung off my dressing-gown, and refilling our glasses with champagne I happily joined my companion in the tub.

CHAPTER TWO

House of Ill Repute

It was later in the day that my hostess revealed to me that indeed the house in which I found myself was not, in fact, an hotel. Welcome though I was to its specialized trade, even to dropping by and passing the time of day and reading the newspapers in the drawing-room, if such were my pleasure, if, in fact, I wanted a place to stay and have a room of my own, I had better check in at one of the more formal hostelries of the town, of which there was a choice.

This I did, and with some relief, I must admit, for pleasant though my welcome had been to the town of Calgary, it was nevertheless an experience which, in retrospect, I found a little embarrassing. Though I must admit at the same time, that my spirits were lifted by a renewed sense of manhood.

On stepping out of the Hotel Windsor the following morning, the air was clear and balmy for a winter's day. I found the main street already quite busy with passersby, noting the sober winter clothing of the women I took to be housewives, the more flamboyant appearance of the ladies of leisure, dark-skinned Indians in furs and mukluks, dog-teams of plume-tailed huskies pulling loaded sleighs piled high with provisions for the trail, and skillfully handled by parka-clad figures who by a single shouted word or the crack of a long whip, guided the eager, intelligent animals through the crowd.

As I stood there surveying the scene, there was a jingle of bells, and a smart sleigh approached, drawn by two fine-looking bay horses. Behind the driver, wrapped in furs, sat Polly Perkins, the proprietress of the "hotel" in which I had been so well received. With every evidence of good cheer, she smiled and nodded to male members of the passing throng, calling out occasionally in a most friendly manner to those on the sidewalk, as if they were intimate acquaintances of hers. She caught my eye, smiled broadly and waved at me, all in the same instant, telling the driver of the sleigh to stop.

The noble horses were reigned in, snorting and blowing steam in the frosty air, jingling the bells on their harness.

"Hullo there! Doctor Watson, is it not?"

In the morning light, I might have expected to see the raddled, middle-aged features of a courtesan beyond her prime, rouged and made up in a vain effort to arrest the passage of time, and of excess. But no — a fresh visage presented itself, comely and intelligent. Her manner was forward, rough perhaps, as befitted the community. I raised my hat.

"Good morning, madame. I trust you are well."

"Indeed I am, Doctor. Can I give you a lift?" Her voice was melodious, if a trifle strident.

"Are you going my way, madame?"

"Which way are you going?"

"To the barracks of the Mounted Police, madame."

"That is precisely where I am going. Please — get in."

She moved over, and I climbed in beside her. Deftly she shared the fur rug with me, spreading it over my lap, and tucking me in with solicitude.

"There," she said, smiling at me. And the sleigh pulled away with a smooth gliding motion, narrowly avoiding a passing dog-team.

"Fine horses," I said, after a moment.

"I get them from the Mounted Police," she replied. "It is a convenient arrangement. I give the horses a little exercise, and I get to use them for free. That is —" she shot me an amused side-glance, "— almost for free."

"Ah," I said in a noncommittal voice.

"A live and let live arrangement," went on the lady. "The fact is that there are a great many lonely men — coal miners, railroad workers, prospectors, cattle-men, who go through this town without a place to call their own, except the brothel. There are many upright citizens who would close us down —"

"And the police?" I ventured.

"They find it better to keep an open understanding in the matter. I keep a clearing house for information which the police find helpful. We behave ourselves, and the police largely wink at us. Except for the odd raid, which I hear about before it occurs." She smiled at me sweetly.

Our swift passage over the snow had led us to the North West Mounted Police barracks, on the edge of the town. The Union Jack flew over low buildings built of logs, which sat in a parade square, it in turn defined by a stockade reminiscent of military arrangements I had experienced in India. The stockade had embrasures and loop-holes, undoubtedly designed to direct defensive rifle-fire, though against whom such fire would now be directed, was an unanswered question.

In the square a curious exercise was in progress, and we stopped to watch. A dozen mounted officers sat astride their horses in a motionless line. Another six or eight police on horseback, starting at the far end of the barracks yard, came galloping in a ragged manner, full tilt towards the silent assembly, clods of mud, snow, and ice flying from their hooves.

These attackers behaved in the most curious fashion, hollering like savages, waving sticks and pieces of colored cloth, as they approached the rigid phalanx in a most threatening manner, changing their flying course only at the last moment to avoid collision.

The marauders had no sooner retired than a bugle sounded and the rigid ranks relaxed. Friendly conversation broke out. Riders dismounted, and walked their horses towards the stables. More than one well-set up police constable caught the eye of my hostess, and came over to pass the time of day, saluting in a most correct fashion. But no sooner had they entered into conversation, than they jumped again to rigid attention at the approach of a more senior officer, a man fully six feet three inches in height, with a torso like an oak tree.

The newcomer gave us an easy salute, probing blue eyes under grizzled brows, a friendly smile in a strong, weathered face. He took the gloved hand of my escort in his own huge paw.

"Greetings, madame. How is business?"

"Well, thank you, superintendent."

The blue eyes turned to me.

"Doctor Watson, I believe."

"Yes, I am Doctor Watson."

... full tilt ...

"We were expecting you. I am Superintendent Steele." The fine fellow introduced himself, thrusting out his hand and taking mine in his huge grip.

"Yes. I got your message, Superintendent," I replied.

"I shall leave you gentlemen, then," said Polly Perkins. "I have business to attend to. Bye bye, Superintendent Steele," she cried in melodious tones. "Thank you for your fine horses." She turned to me and smiled sweetly, "I'm sure we will see *you* again, Doctor Watson." With which parting shot she tapped her driver on the shoulder, and the sleigh moved smoothly away.

In the officers' mess, my outer garments removed, I was offered a glass of good Spanish sherry by a steward in a white mess-jacket.

"Good health," said Superintendent Steele, raising his glass.

I reciprocated, and we drank together, standing comfortably in front of a great fieldstone fireplace in which pine logs were blazing. The room, built of great treetrunks, seemed familiar. I suppose it was the snap and polish of this male fraternity in which I found myself, the clink of spurs, and the imposed orderliness reminiscent of my best days in the Punjab.

"That display of horsemanship was most impressive, Superintendent," I observed.

"Big Bear seems to find it so, Doctor Watson."

"Big Bear?"

"The current Indian chief in these parts. We have periodic meetings with him. Hundreds of braves in feathers and war-paint, all eager to show what fine fellows they are. They try to stampede us from time to time, and as representatives of Her Majesty, we are obliged to demonstrate dignity and control."

I was about to enquire further, when an inner door opened, and two or three uniformed officers entered, accompanied by a familiar figure, dressed quite formally for this wintry weather, with a black morning coat and a nicely tied foulard at his neck.

"Hullo Watson. Nice to see you." It was my old friend, Sherlock Holmes.

I am growing quite used to Holmes turning up in unexpected places. I have discovered more than once that it is not entirely a matter of coincidence. Indeed, there are times when I take what I believe to be an independent action, only to discover that I am following a path that if it has not been set out for me, at least proves to be coincidental with a matter that is concurrently occupying the attention of Sherlock Holmes. So that, whether I wish it or not, I am caught up in yet another Sherlockian adventure.

I find that I am quite ambivalent about this. On one hand, I must admit that, in the first place, learning of the supposed death of my dear friend in the Reichenbach Falls distressed me more deeply than I can say, and necessitated a re-evaluation of my life without him, no sooner had I determined to get on with my own affairs, and to be, as it were, on my own, than his return threw me into a veritable maelstrom of emotional indecision.

And so it has persisted. I seek my independence, and yet I am happiest when I am involved with whatever Holmes has on his plate.

"Hullo Holmes, dear fellow. What brings you here?"

"Inspector Hargreaves."

"I thought Hargreaves was in New York."

"He is. I visited him after the Niagara Falls affair. His contacts extend across the continent."

"Yes?"

"Indian affairs, railway disputes, cattle rustling, rum-running, the settling of old scores between English, Métis and French, not to mention the North and the South — a score of fascinating subjects."

"But why here?"

Holmes caught the bright blue eye of Superintendent Steele.

"I admit to a certain romantic fascination with the N.W.M.P.," he said.

Steele twirled the points of his heavy mustache between finger and thumb. The orderly appeared in his white jacket.

"Sherry, Holmes?" asked Steele.

"Thank you, Superintendent," said Holmes.

Holmes helped himself from the silver regimental tray, and Steele turned to me.

"Actually, Doctor Watson, hearing from Hargreaves that Holmes was on this side of the Atlantic, we invited him to visit. His arrival coincides with a nice problem we have."

I was aware that the other officers in the room were paying attention to our conversation, and that in a curiously intent way they were looking at *me*.

"I hear you had a most pleasant reception when you arrived in town," said Steele in a conversational tone.

"Yes, I did actually," I said, somewhat warily.

"Polly Perkins is noted for her hospitality."

"I discovered that."

I was growing a little embarrassed at this public disclosure of this particular aspect of my private life, an aspect, moreover, into which I had fallen by accident rather than by intention.

"Perhaps whilst you are here you would like to further your acquaintance with her." Steele sipped his sherry and looked at me quizzically over the rim of his glass. "And certain of her customers, perchance," he added.

I was a bit nettled at this suggestion.

"Actually, the purpose of my visit here, Superintendent Steele, was to discover the whereabouts and condition of one of your officers," said I, with as forthright a manner as I could muster.

Steele seemed somewhat surprised at my remark. "One of my officers?" he queried.

"Yes. A certain Reginald C. Braithwaite, from Essex, England. His father is concerned for him. He has not been in touch for some time."

"Ah! Braithwaite!" Steele finished his sherry, and depositing the empty glass gently upon a nearby table, he thoughtfully smoothed his mustache. "Look here, Watson, why do we not go into luncheon, and talk about it." He turned to Holmes and together we moved into the staff dining room.

This was the first time I had sat at an officers' mess since my days in India. I found myself amongst well set-up young men from various backgrounds. Some had served in other parts of the Empire, others had marched a thousand miles westward from Ontario, as part of the force to confront the Riel Rebellion. Still others had left England in search of the romance of the North Western frontier. But of Reggie Braithwaite there was no sign.

"About Polly Perkins' establishment," said Superintendent Steele. "We have reason to believe that it is being used as a rendezvous for certain disruptive elements in the community."

"Is it not within your authority to close the place down, then?" I queried.

"Ah yes. But that would not eliminate the problem. It would only send it underground, and make it more difficult to keep a finger on it. As you may have noticed, Doctor Watson, we have a friendly working relationship with Madame Perkins at the moment."

"Can she not help you, then?"

"She can only observe and report occasionally. We need someone to get directly involved with the rascals."

"Surely your men are trained in such matters, Superintendent."

"My men are excellent, Doctor. But they are all too well known in this community."

I turned to Holmes. "Holmes?"

My friend was filling his pipe with tobacco. He lit it and puffed out clouds of smoke. "It would appear that you have already made an impression on Madame Perkins' entourage, Watson. I must compliment you."

He looked at me through his cloud of tobacco smoke, his eyes veiled. There are times when, in spite of the many years we have spent together in close friendship, I cannot tell what is on Holmes' mind, or indeed of his emotional response to a given situation. I do know of his seeming aversion to women.

"The fair sex is your department," he informed me on one occasion, and yet I have seen him be most charming to the ladies, when it suited him.

Superintendent Steele twisted the waxed ends of his mustache. "Doctor Watson," he said. "You happen to be in a most favourable position for our investigation. And we would much appreciate your assistance in this matter."

"The matter?" I said. "What, pray, is this matter, may I ask."

In the past, I have been a willing accessory to Holmes' adventures, and have been privileged to record them and have them published. But more and more I find myself drawn into active participation in those adventures, somewhat to my increasing discomfort.

"What I had in mind was that you use your reputation at the Perkins establishment to gain access to, and the confidence of, the disruptive element I have mentioned."

"Good lord, sir, can you not be more specific?" I cried.

"I am sorry, I cannot," replied Steele. "The Riel Rebellion has left a current of unrest. The Indians are paupers in their own land. There are cattle thieves and whisky smugglers, rogues and confidence men. We keep our ears to the ground to hear the reverberations, and to control them the best we are able. We are asking you to help."

"What could I possibly do?" said I.

"You could play the part of an English ne'er-do-well, a gambler, a man of good family down on his luck looking for an opportunity to recoup his fortunes — not an unusual character in these parts. How are you at cards?"

"Not very skilled."

"Good. A natural mark!"

Through all this, Holmes sat quietly smoking his pipe and listening to the conversation.

"What is your role in all this, may I ask, Holmes?"

"It really depends upon how it develops, my dear fellow," he replied. It seemed to me that this response was not inconsistent with the manner in which Holmes frequently awaited the denouement of many a specific case he was working on, before being good enough to enlighten me. "I shall certainly follow the proceedings with keen interest, you may be assured Watson."

I had to be satisfied with that. Another thought occurred to me. "It must be general knowledge to anyone that is interested, that I have been interviewed by the police. Will that not alert your mysterious opponents?"

"A newcomer into the community is often checked out by the police, as a matter of course," said Steele. "It will give you a certain cachet!"

Later, as I left the barracks, I realized that I was no closer to the whereabouts of Reggie Braithwaite.

CHAPTER THREE

A Man Called Zack

As I entered Polly Perkins' establishment that evening, I found the place quiet enough. Two or three "ladies of the evening" sat idly at their tables awaiting customers. A man in a loud checked suit, a bowler hat perched on the back of his head, sat at the piano rendering some music hall ballad, and one of the girls leaned over his shoulder, singing along with him.

On my previous visit, I had noticed the informal manner in which the "regulars" entered the establishment and sat themselves down, perhaps picking up a newspaper or a magazine, as if they were comfortably ensconced in their own home. One of the girls would approach, and suggest something from the bar. The man would acquiesce, and presently find himself with a glass of whisky, and perhaps a glass of champagne for the lady. Whether the "champagne" in such a case was genuine or not was open to speculation. On this occasion, the girl that approached me was blonde and buxom.

"Ullo, ducks," she said.

"London, eh?" I said.

"Coo! 'Ow did you know that?" She evinced astonishment in her baby blue eyes, and her rouged lips pursed in the caricature of a smile.

"Bow Bells," I said.

"Well, I never!" She made a move to sit in my lap. I accommodated her.

"My name's Daisy," she said. "Wot's yours?"

"John," I said. "John Watson."

At this, she glanced around the room furtively. "Not Doctor Watson?"

"That's right," I said.

"There was a bloke in 'ere earlier, asking after you," she whispered in my ear.

"Oh? What sort of a bloke?"

"A narsty looking bloke, I 'aven't seen before. 'E said 'e'd be back. Look 'ere, duckie, can't I get you something to drink?"

"Whisky," I said. "And something for yourself." I tucked a two dollar bill into her generous décolleté and she slid off my lap.

"Be right back," she said, and vanished into the next room.

No sooner had she gone than the outer door opened, and with a blast of cold air, three men entered the establishment. As if on a signal the remaining girls in the room stood up with cries of apparent delight. They took hats and coats from two of the men, and hung the garments on wall-hooks. The third newcomer, a dark, sallow fellow, shrugged off their advances. He caught my eye, and advanced upon me.

"Is your name Watson?" he queried.

"It is," I replied.

"Doctor Watson?"

"Correct."

"They call me Zachary. What're you drinkin'?"

"The girl's just bringing me a whisky."

"Good. We'll get a bottle sent up."

"Sent up?"

"To the room. Tell her, will you Harry," he called to one of the other arrivals. "Come on, Doc." With which he marched out of the room, and I dutifully followed.

I noticed that the pianist had turned to see what was going on. His hands had left the keys, but still the instrument continued to play. It was then I noticed his feet pushing the pedals under the instrument. It was a player piano, the melody activated by a roll of paper, which, pierced with holes, gave an acceptable though strident performance. The man himself, in his checked suit, his black walrus mustache, and bowler hat on the back of his head, I recognized with relief, was Sherlock Holmes.

Zachary stood aside to allow me to precede him up the stairs.

"What is this all about?" I asked.

"Hold your horses, an' you'll find out," replied my companion abruptly.

Gaining the landing, we proceeded to the door of the same room I had previously occupied. Zachary gave a soft double knock on the door. There was the sound as of a bolt being withdrawn, and the door opened. I found myself confronting the flushed and comely visage of Colette, my earlier female acquaintance. We entered and the door was closed and locked behind us.

On the bed lay a slender, well-formed young man with an air of elegance about him. His clothing was dishevelled, his fair hair plastered on his brow. He was unconscious, and from his shoulder oozed a dark red stain. I felt the young man's brow, and took his pulse.

"A high temperature, and a low pulse," I said. "And what appears to be a bullet-wound in his body. This young man needs immediate medical attention."

"That's why you're here, Doc," said Zachary.

At this moment, there came a knock on the door.

"Who is it?" cried Zachary.

"Your whisky, sir," replied a female voice.

Zachary unlocked the door, and opened it wide enough to allow a bottle of whisky to be passed through. "Right," he said. The door was closed again, and bolted. The female's footsteps receded.

"I have no instruments, no sedative, no antiseptic, no bandages," I said.

Zachary tossed me the bottle of whisky. "Sedative and antiseptic," he said. From his belt he pulled a keen-bladed Bowie knife. "Instrument." With the point of the knife he lifted the lady's petticoats. "Bandages," said Zachary. Colette blushed, but stood her ground.

It was Afghanistan all over again, mending torn human flesh with inadequate resources.

"I think you should call in the local doctor," I said.

"The local doctor's in cahoots with the police. And they'd be on us like a ton of bricks."

I hesitated, not knowing how far I should play this game.

"Perhaps this will help convince you," said Zachary, and from his coat-tails he pulled what appeared to be a raw-hide tobacco pouch. It weighed heavily in his hand. "Gold dust," he said. I paused. "Or this, if needs be." I looked up and saw the gleam of a revolver in his hand. "Time's a-wasting, Doctor Watson," said Zachary.

Colette had already made up the fire, and on it was a steaming pan of hot water. I took off my jacket, and rolled up my sleeves.

"Can you give me a hand, Colette?" I said.

It was all very well for Superintendent Steele to outline to me his problems of policing this part of the world, and I had been somewhat reassured at the appearance of Holmes in his role as a piano playing roué. But I was uneasy in my ethical position here, of being obliged to conduct an impromptu surgical operation, with a loaded revolver in my back, and a bag of gold dust in my pocket. Also, I was worried about the young man. After the operation, I had been escorted back to my hotel by one of Zachary's men, and told to keep my mouth shut. That was two days ago, and I had heard nothing since.

I recalled the words of Superintendent Steele to me. "You could play the part of an English ne'er-do-well, a gambler looking for an opportunity to recoup his fortunes." And with this thought in mind, I returned to Polly Perkins' establishment, the bag of gold dust in my pocket.

It is difficult to know how informed are the girls in such a place. In the intimacy of the bedroom, surely the most hardened cowboy of the prairies, or the most cosseted town dweller, is equally vulnerable, and will disclose private thoughts which would never pass his lips in less intimate circumstances. The two occasions I had been here had been intimate in more ways than one, so I entered, expecting at least some display of familiarity, perhaps Colette, or Polly herself, with some intimate secret to share. But no, it was as if I were accepted as a member of a club, free to come and go, and to partake of its privileges if I cared to do so.

I ordered a whisky, lit up a stogy and sat in a corner where I could watch the action, as the Americans would say. One of the girls was operating the player-piano. There were two card-tables in operation, with cowboys in black slouch hats and red neckerchiefs, playing with others I was beginning to recognize as "city dudes." The rest of the room was filled with couples coming and going, and two or three girls sitting quietly by themselves. One was knitting, a quiet smile on her face.

"A busy night."

It was a "dude," looking up from a nearby table as he shuffled a deck of cards. The air reeked with cigar smoke.

"It would seem so," I replied. I took a swallow of my whisky.

"English, eh?"

"Yes."

"Care to get in the game?"

"What are you playing?"

"Blackjack."

Blackjack was one card game I was quite familiar with, as I have mentioned elsewhere. "Twenty-one," we called it, sailing around the Horn, crossing the Line and picking up the Northern Trade Winds, homeward bound fc r England.

"Sure."

They made room for me, I sat down and the cards were dealt. The bets were modest. I was dealt a good hand and I won.

"Hey. The guy's lucky!"

I won again, and the bets went up. Then the tide turned, and though I was no tyro to the game, I lost repeatedly. It was not my intention to lose, rather to establish myself as a vulnerable English ne'er-do-well gambler, and await developments. They were not long in coming.

"Hey, what are you guys doin'?"

I looked up, and Zachary was standing beside the table, his hat on the back of his head, cheroot in mouth, hands thrust into his jacket pockets.

"Hiya, Zack. Havin' a friendly game."

"Friendly game, my foot."

"What d'ya mean?"

"I can see the elastic stickin' out from here!" He reached over, and taking one of the men by the collar, he pulled him up and shook him vigorously. Two aces and a jack fell out of the fellow's sleeves. "Give the guy back 'is money. He's a friend of mine."

"Just a joke, Zack. No offense, fella."

The men disgorged their take and dispersed sheepishly. Zachary sat down beside me, giving me a smile which reminded me of sharks I had seen in the Red Sea, basking in the sun.

"You need someone to look after you, Doc," he said, and he waved to one of the girls for more whisky. "It's like this," he said. "That little bag of gold I gave you for your services the other day —?"

"Yes. How's my patient?"

"He's doin' fine. Thanks to you."

"Where is he?"

"He's okay.... Like I said. The gold...."

"Yes?"

"There's lots more where that came from."

"Oh?"

The whisky arrived. "Good health," said my companion. "And good fortune?" He put a query on the end of his observation.

"Good luck," I said, ready to follow wherever the conversation seemed to lead. We drank, and Zachary looked at me with his dark eyes.

"You look to me like an Englishman of the professional classes, down on his luck, seeking his fortune in the colonies. Am I right?"

"More or less," I muttered.

"With something in his past that he would just as soon forget, perhaps."

"Right again," I said, and took a gulp of my whisky. It is interesting, that, called upon to play a part, I see myself entering into it as if indeed it were real. So it was on this occasion. After a whisky or two.

"The matter of fortune," said Zachary.

"Yes?"

"The opportunities in this land are sitting there ready to be taken."

"I wish I could find them," said I.

"Opportunity," he said. "What have you got to offer?"

"Me?" I replied. "Very little. Medicine only, I suppose. Even that is questionable at times."

"Yet with medicine you can save lives," he said. Then quietly, he added, "Or take them."

"Take lives!" I said. I met his eye with indignation. "That's hardly in accord with the Hippocratic Oath!" I choked back my disapproval of the fellow.

"True enough, Doc," he toyed with his whisky. "But isn't it interesting how we change our position on this question? During a war, we will bend every effort to destroy our enemy by every means in our power, while at the same time adhering to an ethic that to kill one's fellow being is a mortal sin. Have you figured that out, Doc?"

I had a vivid flash of bloody memory from the Afghan conflict. "No, I have not."

"Well then, I'll tell you what I've arrived at."

"Yes?"

"That if it's okay for the government of one's country to declare war on another country for its own gain, then it is similarly all right for the individual to do the same thing for his own benefit."

I looked at him in astonishment. "You try it here, and you will have the law on your neck!" I cried.

"Who is it that said the law is an ass?" He grinned at me over his glass.

"Dickens, I think."

"Well there you go, then," he exclaimed. "Listen, Doc, mebbe we can get together, you and me." He gulped back his drink, rose from his chair, and leaned over me, with his black eyes and wolfish grin. "Just watch out for these cheap card sharps, and the lovely ladies." With which he left me.

Back at my hotel, I had no sooner gone to my room and taken off my coat, than there came a discreet tap at the door. I opened it, and there was Holmes, looking well set up against the cold in a fur coat and hat.

"Holmes!" I cried, pleased to see him. "Do come in."

"My dear Watson," he said, entering. "I am sorry we haven't been more in touch." He closed the door securely, removed his outer clothing, and felt for his pipe. "How was the denouement with the fellow Zachary?"

"The 'denouement,' as you call it, Holmes, was an impromptu operation at gun point in a harlot's bedroom."

"Constable Reggie Braithwaite," said Holmes. He had lit his pipe, and tobacco fumes curled around his head.

"What's that you say, Holmes?"

"The young man you operated upon was Reginald Braithwaite. Working as an undercover agent for the police. At last report," he added.

"Good Lord!" I cried. "I have been hunting for him for months, with a message from his father, back in England — "

"How was he?" asked Holmes.

"Unconscious. A bullet in his shoulder. I patched him up. Here," I rummaged in my pocket. "Here's the bullet I dug out." I passed the piece of lead over to Holmes, who whipped out his magnifying glass to examine it.

"Hm, 38 calibre," he grunted. "A police weapon."

"A police officer under cover, shot by the police themselves," I cried.

"Possibly." He held up the fragment of lead between slender finger and thumb. "May I keep this?"

"Of course, Holmes." He put the bullet in his pocket.

"I can't get over it, I must say. Reggie Braithwaite! Nice young chap, by the look of him."

"So Zachary had a gun in your ribs," observed Holmes. "Any other inducement?"

"Yes, in fact. Since you ask." I felt in the pocket of my discarded overcoat, and produced the little chamois bag. I dropped it in Holmes' outstretched hand. "Gold," I said.

"Ah," said Holmes. "The plot thickens."

"It does indeed, Holmes." He loosened the drawstrings on the little bag, and its contents glittered dully under the kerosene lamp. "There is what I take to be an identifying mark, stamped into the chamois," I went on. "Perhaps you can make out what it is. I can't make head or tail of it."

Holmes carried the bag closer to the lamp, and took out his magnifying glass a second time.

"It looks like a hedgehog," I offered.

"A porcupine," said Holmes.

"Ah."

"A recent gold strike in the vicinity of Cardston, Alberta. Porcupine Gulch. It is one of the matters currently concerning the N.W.M.P. It may turn out to be a strike as big as Barker Creek, with the same influx of desperadoes and outlaws from the Barbary Coast."

"And it would appear that Zachary is one of the first on the scene."

"Along with Reggie Braithwaite," observed Sherlock Holmes.

"Reggie?" I queried. "Surely —" I paused. "Surely he is not in with Zachary?"

"It has happened before," said Holmes. "The same instinct that has drawn an adventurous young fellow into the Force, can equally well attract him to less noble endeavours." He weighed the chamois bag in his hand. "The contents of this little bag could represent perhaps six months pay to an N.W.M.P. constable. Also, what was Zachary's motivation in saving the life of your Reggie Braithwaite, unless he has need of him?"

"It would be a great disappointment to Reggie's family," I said, "were he to stray like that."

"I'm sure it would, Watson." Holmes looked at me with a faint smile, perhaps a little amused at my streak of sentiment. True, cold reason, I reminded myself, Holmes placed above all things, sentiment included.

"I must be getting back to the barracks," he said. "Is there anything else I should know?"

"Yes. Zachary seems to accept me as a possible associate, as a doctor with shifty morals," I said in somewhat bitter tones. "He says he will be in touch."

"Good," said Sherlock Holmes. He donned his hat and coat, and flung a scarf around his neck. "I'm taking the gold with me, Watson. It will be of considerable interest to the authorities, have no doubt, and probably be evidence in due course." With which he tightened the drawstrings of the little bag, and put it in his pocket.

"Good night to you, Watson."

So saying he left, and I thought with a touch of regret how the contents of that little chamois bag would have improved my dwindling resources. Alas.

CHAPTER FOUR

I Become a Remittance Man

I awakened the following morning, pushing the blankets off my bed. The temperature, it seemed, had risen considerably during the night. I crossed to the window of my hotel bedroom. The snow of yesterday was melting and water was running in the street, turning it to mud. It was the "Chinook" — the mild wind which in these parts could raise the temperature as much as fifty degrees in a few hours. With it I was aware of the hoarse bellow of cattle, and past my window came a stream of wild-eyed cattle-beasts, hundreds of them, it seemed, tossing their heads, and protesting vigorously, as cowboys in black hats and raw-hide "chaps" — sort of leather pantalons worn as protection for their nether regions — used their lariats and hoarse cries to shepherd the animals down the street towards the railway siding.

In Canada's Western provinces, as in the American West, certain elements had come together to encourage ranching. The prairie, now virtually denuded of the buffalo, provided forage for thousands of head of cattle. The newly established railway provided transportation to the eastern markets, and the generous local deposits of coal provided ready fuel for the trains to transport the beasts to these markets.

Amongst the cowboys, I recognized two or three I had seen at Polly Perkins' establishment. They straddled their mounts as if born in the saddle. Unlike their English counterparts, the fraternity of landed gentry "riding to hounds," these fellows moved as if one with the horse. The saddle was quite differently designed, with a great "pommel" around which one could pass the "lariat" or "lasso," which at times was used to restrain a rebellious cattle-beast.

Watching the passing throng, I became aware of a figure on a fine stallion rather than a little cow-pony.

He wore a black Stetson hat pulled over his brow, and smoked a long thin cigar. He seemed to be a sort of overseer, a person of authority. As he came close, he turned to check the passage of the beleaguered beasts. It was Zachary.

It was then that I was aware of a knock on my bedroom door. I was still in my pyjamas.

"Just a minute."

I threw on my dressing-gown, and unlocked the door. An N.W.M.P. constable stood there, bright of eye, and exuding robust good health. He stood at attention.

"Doctor Watson, sir!"

"Yes, constable."

"Compliments of Superintendent Steele sir, and he would like to see you at your earliest convenience."

Superintendent Steele stood up and came from behind his desk and greeted me cheerfully, his highly polished Sam Browne belt and his officers' boots gleaming in the morning rays of the sun coming through the barracks window.

"Sorry to call you so early in the day, Doctor."

"Not a bit, Superintendent," I replied.

Holmes was standing with his back to the fire.

"Good morning, Holmes."

"Morning, Watson."

"There has been a development," said Steele. An orderly entered, served us coffee and withdrew.

"Yes?" I said.

"And you are in the middle of it, dear fellow," said Holmes cheerfully. "You and the fellow Zachary."

"Oh," I said. The coffee was hot and bitter. I added sugar and sat myself down.

"Cattle, guns, and gold," said Steele, He rolled the waxed points of his mustache between finger and thumb.

"I saw cattle on the move this morning," I said. "Right down the main street past my hotel. Zachary appeared to be in charge." I sipped my coffee and glanced at Holmes, wondering what his role was in this business.

"Zachary pays American ranchers in gold, brings cattle across the border and sells them on contract to the Eastern markets. Quite aboveboard," Steele went on.

"You mentioned guns," I said.

"Yes, I did," replied Steele. "These are turbulent times in the West, Doctor. The half-breed Riel was hanged just a few years ago for fomenting revolution, and many of his followers still harbour a keen resentment against the authorities for that action. There are dissident Blackfeet, unhappy with their lot, despite their pledge of loyalty to Queen Victoria. The buffalo have vanished from the prairie, the land is fenced in, the railway brings in more and more settlers, the original inhabitants are squeezed into reservations. It is no wonder that at times they seek to break out of their bonds. Zachary is one of those rascals who seek to exploit these conditions."

I looked over at Holmes, now seated in an easy chair, eyes hooded, seemingly occupied with his own thoughts.

"Holmes tells me that Zachary had you perform an emergency operation at the Perkins' establishment," said Steele.

"Yes," I replied.

"At pistol point, I am informed."

"That's correct. I had little choice. The patient, it turned out, was none other than Reggie Braithwaite, the young fellow that I was looking for on behalf of his concerned father back in England. One of your men, I was led to believe, Superintendent."

"That's correct, one of my men," said Steele frowning. "Did you communicate with him?"

"No, I did not. He was not conscious at the time."

"I see," said Steele thoughtfully. He sat down behind his desk and finished his coffee. "I must confide in you, gentlemen," he said. "There are times when members of the North West Mounted Police are subjected to considerable temptation. A recruit like young Braithwaite, for instance: intelligent, adventurous, a fellow of good family who has seen much of the world; now in the service of the Queen, paid a veritable pittance to carry out the arduous duties of a frontier policeman. In the process of upholding the law, such a man may come into contact with a man like Zachary, and be subjected to temptation. Zachary is a legitimate cattle-dealer, but there are also rumours of arms shipments, and of deals with restive Indians, in return for considerable amounts of gold.

"On occasion, gentlemen, one mounts an undercover operation to get to the bottom of such rumours, and I appointed young Braithwaite to that task. But I must confess, I am not sure at this point, whether

Braithwaite knows where his duty lies. What are your thoughts in the matter, Holmes?"

Holmes opened his eyes, and blew a plume of smoke into the air. "With due respect, Superintendent, I am just a visitor passing through, curious as to police methods here in the Canadian West, but hardly one to offer solutions to matters I know little of."

"Matters, indeed!" Steele poured himself more coffee. "Coffee, Watson? Holmes?" He refreshed our cups, and sat again at his desk. "As I have indicated, gentlemen, this is a time of change in the Canadian West. And not the least of the problem are rascals like Zachary who seek personal gain amidst the turbulence. It is my responsibility here, gentlemen, in these difficult times, to 'maintain the right.'"

"If I may make an observation, Superintendent?" Holmes lay back in his easy chair, smoke wreathing up from his pipe.

"Indeed, Holmes," said Steele.

"Watson's introduction into Polly Perkins' establishment," said Holmes, "and his excellent service to this fellow Zachary, has put him, I would suggest, in a position which could be most useful to you, Superintendent, and the splendid force in which you serve. 'Maintain the right' indeed! Am I not correct, sir?" The smoke from his pipe floated round his brow.

"Quite correct, Holmes," replied Steele.

My feelings sank as the keen-eyed police officer turned his attention towards me. After all, Holmes was supposed to be the man of action, not me!

"As you may have observed, Doctor," said Steele, "Madame Perkins' establishment is frequented by a wide range of habitués. Decent fellows, many of them, far from home, railway workers, frontier cowboys looking for a little warmth in their lonely lives. Some are less salubrious fellows, card sharps and rascals, living by their wits."

I sat there, feeling that circumstances beyond my control once again were sweeping me away.

"Polly Perkins' place, I may say, is a clearing house for information useful to us in maintaining law and order in this district. Polly herself is helpful to us, in return for certain courtesies. But you have already observed this, I'm sure." I remembered the handsome gelding that had brought me to the barracks. "Then there is Zachary. We placed young Braithwaite as a ne'er-do-well remittance man, to keep an eye on him. We did not hear from Braithwaite until he turned up at Madame Perkins' establishment with a bullet in his shoulder."

I was aware of both Steele and Holmes looking at me as if awaiting my response.

"Yes?" I said, without enthusiasm.

"It is my considered opinion, Doctor Watson, that you could be of inestimable assistance in this matter, with the reputation you have already built in the community."

"Reputation?" I repeated blankly.

"Madame Perkins has informed me that you are already recognized locally as a doctor of considerable skill."

"That is kind of her," I responded.

"But of dubious reputation."

"Oh," I said.

"That you are out here on Canada's frontier, like many other down-at-the-heel Englishmen, seeking your fortune in whatever way presents itself. Honest or otherwise."

I felt my face flush. Not infrequently in my association with Holmes, I have willingly set aside certain of my medical responsibilities in order to assist him. But the role of a doctor "of dubious reputation" was a part I was not eager to play.

I sat silent for some moments. Holmes regarded me through lowered lids and tobacco fumes. Superintendent Steele had stuffed his own briar full of tobacco, and lighting a match, was soon wreathed in his own cloud of smoke. In a way I felt that these two eminent upholders of law and order had conspired to entrap me, and I did not like the sensation.

From the parade ground came the click of heels and the stamp of booted feet, in response to the barked orders of a young adjutant, and for a moment I was carried back to my own duties on the frontier of India. Another time, another place.

"What more do you want me to do?" I queried.

CHAPTER FIVE

The Perils of Headless Valley

I became quite an habitué of Polly Perkins' Place, and quite a hand at blackjack and five-card stud. My earlier association with Zachary had not gone unnoticed, and in consequence there was largely an absence of trickery from even the most seasoned card sharps. Instead, as a doctor, I was taken into the confidence of many of the habitués, both male and female, revealing tales of fortitude, courage and tragedy, in that community of souls, so far removed from the amenities of civilization.

The balmy Chinook winds continued to blow, and the snow continued to melt. Early one afternoon, a rangy fellow entered the Perkins' establishment, leather chaps on skinny legs, a sheepskin jacket on his back, a sweat-stained Stetson slouch hat pulled over his dark brow. I had not seen him before.

"You Doc Watson?" he grunted.

"Yes I am, actually. What's your name?"

"Beggs. Sam Beggs. There's a horse waitin' fer ya, Doc. Bring yer bag."

"Bag. Right, Mr. Beggs."

I pocketed the few gains I had made at the card-table, and finished my drink. My card-playing companions had stopped talking, and they covertly eyed the dark newcomer. The usual hubbub of conversation in the establishment had faded to silence, and only the player-piano jangled on with some music-hall tune. I followed the man out, and the buzz of conversation was resumed behind us.

"Er — what about clothes? I'm not dressed for horseback riding."

"Zack'll fix you up."

"Oh. I'll get my bag."

It was mild in the Chinook thaw. Two dark horses stood by the hitching rail.

"I — er — I haven't ridden a horse for years."

"It's a cow-pony. Just hold on."

"Oh. Right." I climbed on, and sure enough, in the Western saddle, the beast moved under me in a reassuring manner.

We proceeded to the edge of town, to halt presently outside a wooden building which from the front appeared to be two stories, with windows up and down. From the side however, it was apparent that the structure had but one story. The rest of it was obviously a fake front, windows and all, reaching up into the otherwise empty sky. I wondered what quirk of false pride had led the builder to this curious indulgence, not uncommon in these parts.

There was a hitching rail to which two or three horses were already tied. A lithe form moved from the shadows, a silent, dark-visaged Indian on moccasined feet, a single eagle feather in his black braids. We dismounted, and entered the building.

There was a single room, in which a bearskin rug on the floor vied for attention with an Indian mask on the wall, the latter a grinning visage with a lopsided mouth, and great vacant eyes which appeared to follow my passage. Occupying the middle of the room was a well made pine table, with empty chairs and benches; in one corner was a brass bedstead. A pot-bellied wood stove kept the place warm. Rough clothing hung from nails banged in the walls. By the door we had just entered sat two silent Indian figures, their dark hair decorated with eagle plumes.

The door closed behind me, and, medical bag in hand, I approached the bed, expecting to see young Braithwaite, pale and wan, in need of my professional assistance. The bed was empty. Puzzled, I turned to my escort. He was busy taking items of clothing from the wall and flinging them on the table.

"Clothes," he said. "Wool shirt, heavy pants, sheepskin coat. Beaver hat with earmuffs. Heavy boots. Take your pick. You'll need 'em where we're goin'."

"Where are we going?"

"Indian country. In the Rockies."

"And my patient?" I looked around in some bewilderment.

"Thunder Sky's son."

"Thunder Sky?"

"Indian chief. Ogokee tribe. He's holed up in the Headless Valley district."

"What's the matter with his son?"

"That's for you to find out, eh? Get into your bush outfit, and we'll get goin'."

"Zachary and young what's-his-name, Braithwaite?" I was putting on the noisome clothing. "Where are they?"

"They're waitin' for you."

"When last I saw Braithwaite, he had a bullet in his shoulder."

"He seems okay now."

I was consumed with curiosity. I could not believe that Zachary was friendly with a tribal chief and his invalid son simply out of the kindness of his heart. I was reminded of Superintendent Steele's reference to "restive Indians," and rumours of arms shipments in return for gold. I wondered also how I was to communicate my whereabouts and any discovery I might make to Holmes, and indeed how to appeal for help should I need it.

As we emerged from the building, the lithe young Indian was again in attendance, handling our horses and helping load saddlebags and baggage. This activity attracted the attention of a passing carriage, which pulled up, seemingly out of curiosity. Two people were in the carriage. The driver was Polly Perkins, dressed in the height of fashion; with her was an elegant, foppish fellow, who seemed familiar to me.

"I say," cried the latter, in an affected tone of voice. "Is that not my old chum Watson? Good Lord, old man, what are you doing, rigged out like that? Chasing you out of town, are they?" It was Holmes.

"An emergency call," I replied. "Headless Valley, Indian territory."

Zachary was just coming round the house, loaded with saddlebags. Reggie Braithwaite was with him. Zachary looked up sharply as I spoke, and threw his bags across his horse.

"Indian territory?" cried Holmes disdainfully. "Good Lord. And you, one of the finest surgeons in England! What have you come to, old chap?"

"I do my best," I replied. Zachary had turned towards us, curbing his anger.

"Good afternoon, Mr. Zachary," Polly Perkins smiled graciously.

"Ma'am," replied Zachary. He touched the brim of his slouch hat, and glowered at Holmes.

"Good afternoon, Doctor Watson," murmured Polly in gracious tones. "Take care."

"Good afternoon, Madame. I will try to," I said, feeling that I cut a most ungallant figure in my borrowed sheepskins and moth-eaten fur hat.

"Look us up when you get back," called Holmes. Polly Perkins smiled sweetly, and the carriage moved off up the street.

The Indians were already mounted. Braithwaite tightened his saddle girths. Zachary helped me into my saddle. "Who the devil was that guy?" he wanted to know.

"A fellow I knew in London. A rascal if ever there was one."

"What's he doin' here?"

"I've no idea," I said, close in fact to the truth.

Zachary grunted. He mounted his steed. Braithwaite followed his example, and we moved off down the street, I feeling comforted that at least my friend Sherlock Holmes knew where I was going.

With the mild Chinook winds for the past few days, the mountain passes were clear enough of snow to allow our passage on horseback. Easy though the Western saddle was on my posterior, I nevertheless quickly became exhausted at the never-ending movement of my agile mount under me, and after some hours of incessant scrambling up the rocky slopes, I was reduced to little more than a piece of baggage which had the ability to cling tenaciously to the pommel of the saddle.

"How ya doin', Doc?"

At last we had stopped to camp. Our Indian escort had already dismounted, and were flinging up a shelter for the night. The sun had set in a clear sky, suffusing the snowy mountain peaks with gold. Zachary, seeing I had difficulty in dismounting, had come to give me a hand.

"Terrible, thank you." With my host's assistance, I slid off my patient mount, regained my feet, and stretched my weary body. "How is the patient?" I asked.

"Patient?" said Zachary. He was lighting a cheroot, and his dark eyes gleamed at me through the plume of smoke. Beyond him, Reggie Braithwaite was efficiently attending to his horse's needs.

I nodded in his direction. "Braithwaite."

"Oh, him."

Zachary looked across at the young man, little more than a boy, vulnerable, he appeared to me. "He's doin' okay. Good enough for what he's come for, anyways." Zachary grinned to himself, as at a private joke. "You've hardly met 'im, have ya, Doc," he said. "Other than takin' a bullet out of his arm. Hey, Braithwaite," he called, to draw the young man's attention. "Come over here." He waved his arm in a wide gesture.

"Right. Just a minute." The youngster finished unsaddling his horse, and gave it some feed, fondling its muzzle in the process. Then he crossed over to us with an apologetic smile.

"Look after your horse, if you want him to look after you," he said.

"This is Doctor Watson," said Zachary. "The man that operated on you."

"I'm delighted to meet you, Doctor Watson," said Braithwaite with an open smile, thrusting out his hand. "Thank you for your excellent services."

The intonation was English, public school, a little delicate, perhaps, for my taste. His hand-grip was firm and reassuring.

"Has anyone had a look at your shoulder, since I operated?" I queried.

"It's been kept clean with antiseptic you provided, doctor."

"Good. I'd better look at it."

Our Indian companions already had a fire going. "Bannock and beans," said Zachary. "Ten minutes." He grinned at us, cheroot between his teeth, and left us with a parting shot. "Don't you two get into trouble, now. I need you."

I retrieved my medical bag, and sat my patient on a log. In the waning light of day, I unwound the soiled bandage from his shoulder. We were alone. "What did our host mean by his parting remark, do you suppose?"

The boy glanced up at me, shrewdly enough, I thought. As a doctor, the young fellow trusted me. But with nothing more to go on, he also viewed me as an adventurer of dubious background, and was wary in his response.

"Might I ask what he needs you for, doctor?" I was surprised at his apparent ignorance of the stated purpose of our trip.

"There seems to be an Indian child, the son of an important chief, who needs medical attention. Zachary has requested my assistance."

"That's very considerate of Zachary, worrying about the health of an Indian child." There was a note of cynicism in the young man's voice. I had unwound the soiled bandage. The wound was healing nicely. I got some alcohol from my kit.

"Your shoulder's looking all right," I said.

"That's good," replied my patient.

I was aware of Zachary once more approaching us.

"How're ya doing?" he said.

"I'm applying a fresh dressing."

"Hurry it up, then," said Zachary, and he retired.

"What's your function in this, may I ask?" I queried.

"I'm a linguist," replied Braithwaite. "Greek, German, French. Some North American Indian dialects. That's what I'm doing for Zachary. Indian, I mean."

"I thought he talked Indian himself."

"Some dialects, badly. That's why he needs me."

"So that's your role."

"That's it, doctor. But I might add, for your own safety, that with a man like Zachary, you have to watch your every step, whatever your motivation. That's all I can say."

I finished the dressing. The young fellow got to his feet and went to the fire, where Zachary was filling tin plates with food. The Indians were already chewing on what I took to be lumps of pemmican, a mixture of cranberries and buffalo meat, said in these parts to be of great and balanced food value. I wondered briefly where the dried meat had come from, since the buffalo population on the plains had been decimated with the coming of the white man. And I was little further ahead in determining what part young Braithwaite was playing. Was he still an agent for the police, or had he elected to join forces with Zachary with a view to lining his own pockets advantageously?

After the arduous day on the trail, the rough meal of bannock and beans, washed down with quantities of hot tea, satisfied the inner man, and I was most happy to settle down for the night in the down-filled sleeping bag my host was thoughtful enough to supply.

I noticed that after tending to the horses, Braithwaite retired at once, but Zachary conferred haltingly with his Indian guide in some guttural language I did not understand. I saw the Indian with whom Zachary had been speaking confer briefly with his dark companion, before slipping off into the woods, silent as a shadow, the way we had come.

Zachary threw another log on the fire, and checked the pistol he carried on his belt, oiling it and wiping it carefully, and checking the six bullets it contained. He placed it under his folded sheepskin coat which served him as a pillow, before settling down for the night.

It seemed I had barely closed my eyes, when I was aware of my shoulder being shaken, and of Zachary's voice.

"Come on, Doc. Time to move."

"What?" I said, as if drugged. "I've barely closed my eyes!"

"It's dawn."

"Already?"

"Time to go. There's a cup of tea fer you." The crouching figure moved away from me, and I turned over in my sleeping bag, propping myself up on one elbow. The eastern horizon was suffused with pale light. Beside me on the ground was a mug of hot tea, steaming in the cold morning air. I sipped it gratefully, and found it strong and sweet. Somewhere I had heard that those bold voyageurs who opened up this astonishing continent by canoe, wakened the same way, drinking an early morning cup of tea, strong and sweet, then decamping and paddling perhaps fifty extra miles on their journey before stopping for breakfast.

So it was today. There was some cold bannock left over from the previous evening's meal, had I wished to eat it. But our energies were bent on striking camp and moving towards our destination with all speed. The young brave whom I had seen dispatched on his secretive mission the previous evening had rejoined us, and was already packing his gear on his horse, for the forward passage of our journey.

But what was the young man's night time excursion, I wondered. I could only assume that Zachary was wasting no time to get to his destination, before being overtaken. For who knew what rivalries there were on this wild frontier?

Braithwaite had saddled and bridled his horse, and readied his saddlebags and equipment, while I was still fumbling with mine.

"Good morning, doctor. Give you a hand?"

"Thank you very much."

He was already tightening my saddle girth. "Sleep well?" he asked.

"Like a log. How's the shoulder?"

"Never better. We'll just adjust your pack a little. Easier on the horse."

Zachary had noticed Braithwaite's ready assistance and crossed over to us, the brim of his black felt hat pulled down against the rays of the rising sun. His eyes gleamed at me. "I wanta move along, Doc," he said.

"Ready in a minute." Braithwaite helped me into the saddle. "I was just going to ask Braithwaite something," I said.

Zachary glanced at us suspiciously. "What d'you wanta know?" he said.

"How Headless Valley got its curious name."

Zachary responded with a snort of sardonic laughter. "Some say because it just suddenly stops. No head to it, jus' a great jeezly water-fall. Then again I've heard it said there's supposed to be the remains of two gold prospectors up there, tied to a tree. Two skeletons sittin' there with their rusty shovels and pans. An' guess what? Their heads! They got no heads!" He laughed again, a grating sound on the peaceful morning air, showing his teeth in his dark face. "Some guys will do anything fer gold!"

Braithwaite glanced at me as if to gauge my reaction to this grisly information.

"Let's go, eh?" cried Zachary. He swung onto his mount, and was away with a rattle of hooves on the stony trail.

Three days had passed, and I did little more than hang onto the pommel of my saddle, and let the horse pick its way along the narrow trails. At times the way led along precarious heights from which a mis-step, I felt, could precipitate one a thousand feet to the ravine below. At another point, following a narrow gorge, we approached what appeared to be a sheer cliff ascending to the sky, over which dashed a tumultuous waterfall, the rushing stream bursting over the rocks beside us.

As we drew closer, I saw beside our path the ragged remains of an ancient tree, its dead branches reaching out over the raging water. The Indians picked their way around the tree, and then, to my amazement, spurring their horses, they abruptly disappeared into the steaming welter of the falls.

Braithwaite, under instructions from Zachary, was the next to go, and Zachary turned to me, shouting above the roar of the torrent. "Keep right behind me. Your horse will follow mine." With which he set his mount directly against the face of the waterfall, and he too disappeared.

I had but a moment. I had no idea how well Superintendent Steele or his men were acquainted with this remote region. Neither could I know whether they were aware of the passage through the turbulent fall of water, to whatever regions lay beyond.

Quickly I felt in my inner pocket, my hand grasping a visiting card, "John Watson, M.D.," and as my faithful steed passed the tree, I reached out at peril of my balance, and endeavoured to stick the card under a piece of ragged bark to record my passage. Alas, my effort was in vain. The bark failed to hold the card, which fluttered into the torrent and was lost.

CHAPTER SIX

Thunder Sky and Shining Arrow

I was doused briefly under falling water then as my horse carried me onward, I found myself in a rocky chasm which led at an easy gradient into a sunlit glen. The snow had disappeared except on the peaks of the surrounding mountains. There was a warmth in the air, as of approaching spring, and presently, surmounting a grassy rise in the land came half a dozen mounted warriors, armed with bows and arrows, riding at full tilt towards us. As they came, the skilled riders performed extraordinary feats of horsemanship, one moment standing on the bare backs of the galloping horses, the next swinging under the animal's belly in a most agile manner. All the while uttering cries and whoops, which in other circumstances I would have found blood-curdling. This appeared to be a welcome committee for our arrival, as with no slackening of speed, they circled around us two or three times before heading back the way they had come.

This was my first glimpse of the "noble savage," uncontaminated, untouched by the inroads of civilization. My spirits lifted, as if I had been welcomed into a select community of a new and pristine world.

As we proceeded, there were daisies underfoot, and other wild flora springing from the grass; in the air were the scents of spring. I pushed back my moth-eaten fur hat, and loosened my sheepskin jacket. We surmounted the rise in the land, and there below us lay an Indian settlement of gaily painted skin wigwams. Cooking fires sent aromatic fumes into the air. Women went about their business, preparing food, meeting the demands of vociferous children. A hum of happy human voices hung on the air.

Our welcome committee had dismounted, and were formed up beside one of the larger, and more ornately decorated teepees, set a little apart from the rest. We approached, and stopped at a little distance from it. The crowd of women and children clustered forward with smiling curious faces. Our Indian guides exchanged a few words with Zachary and Braithwaite, whereupon they dismounted and proceeded on foot. They entered the teepee, and left us for a few minutes. Presently the older of the two reappeared, and with solemn mien, crossed the intervening space to talk with my companions."

I waited patiently. Then Zachary turned to me. "You go in and see 'im, Doc," he said, a wolfish grin on his face. "Take your little black bag. I've presented you as a great white medicine man. Me and Braithwaite will come with you. He knows their lingo."

"I'll do what I can," I said, climbing stiffly out of my saddle. "Here, take this, would you." I took off my sheepskin coat, too hot for the balmy temperature. I was about to remove my fur hat as well, but with some thoughts of the inappropriateness of being bare headed in such august tribal company, I stayed my hand. I have thought before of the singular importance with which we imbue headgear, from the jewel-encrusted crowns of European royalty to the eagle feathers of the North American Red Indian. I clapped my worn beaverskin cap more firmly on my head, took my black bag in hand, and with Zachary and Braithwaite, was led off through the crowd of concerned and curious onlookers, to the chief's tent.

It was a spacious interior, the skins of which it was made scraped so thin that the translucent light of day glowed through it. On a slightly raised wooden platform lay a handsome youth, emaciated, dark of skin but with a certain pallor, a grayish texture, which I had seen at times in India.

On one side of the couch squatted a figure in grotesque make-up, a painted wooden mask covering his face, dark blood-shot eyes gleaming through sunken eye-sockets, the curved beak of an eagle, perhaps, colored vermilion, as if dipped in blood. As we entered, this creature raised its arms, which at once became wings. It uttered a strange squawk, forbidding, foreboding.

On the other side sat a noble figure, a man perhaps in his sixties, erect, imperious; his bright eyes met mine. His face was lined and creased with the passage of years. His gray hair was plaited, a pair of eagle feathers decorated his scalp, and around his throat and his thin wrists gleamed circlets of shining metal.

"That's gold he's wearin'," said Zachary.

My attention on the patient, I was shocked at this blunt utterance, and turned to Zachary. His eyes glittered with greed. "We are here to save a life," I said. "I suggest we get on with it."

"Yeah," grinned Zachary. "That's what we're here for. Tell 'im, will you, Braithwaite?"

Our young linguist spoke to the chief in a sonorous Indian tongue. The grand old man listened solemnly, and presently, as Braithwaite finished his oration, he replied in courtly, measured cadences. Braithwaite translated for us.

"He, Thunder Sky, chief of the Ogokee, welcomes you as a great medicine man, come to save the life of Shining Arrow, son and future chief of his tribe."

"Tell him that we will do our best," I said, glancing at Zachary, who nodded his approval. At my words, the medicine man raised his wings, and the eagle's beak snapped open in a hiss of apparent disapproval. "And ask him," I went on, "what authority this eagle fellow has in the matter."

There was a rapid interchange of speech with the old man. "He says that the eagle is great medicine, and your medicine added to his will undoubtedly be successful in bringing his son back to life."

I saw that to banish the eagle fellow from the bedside was to make an enemy of him, and I was not interested in losing my scalp, however the operation on my patient turned out. On the other hand, how was I to make use of him in the pursuit of the modern European practice of medicine. I looked the man over, and saw that the eagle wings were attached to his arms in such a manner that at least left his hands free.

An extra pair of hands could be useful. I caught his eyes staring at me through the mask. For want of a suitably significant gesture, I raised my hands, palms together, and facing him I bowed my head in an expression of salutation familiar to me in India.

"Tell them that I welcome the association of their noble Eagle medicine man, and I wish to work with him to cure the young patient. And first of all, I want hot water to wash our hands!"

The orders were swiftly passed, and so far as I could tell, were acceptable. While waiting for the water, I pressed the old chief with further questions. What had led to the semi-conscious condition of his son?

Braithwaite queried Thunder Sky, and received a terse response: "Fall from horse."

"What happened?" I asked.

The old man expanded his response. His son was the best rider in the hard-riding tribe. Gallant, brave, and skilled. Riding after buffalo, he was always in the midst of the action.

"Buffalo?" I asked, surprised.

"That's what he said," replied Braithwaite. "Then the boy took a tumble and banged his head. Since then, he has been in a coma. Ten days."

The hot water had arrived in neatly made birch bark containers; at my instruction, they were set down on the floor. Turning to the old chief and the medicine man, I ceremoniously rolled up my sleeves, capturing their attention. With a flourish, I opened my bag and took out a cake of carbolic soap, and then in the manner of a conjurer, I took the soap between my fingers and dipped it in the hot water. I scrubbed up a lather on my hands, and indicated that the medicine man should do likewise. He hesitated, but as I nodded and smiled encouragement, he took the soap and copied my procedure. When finally his hands were well soaped, I plunged my hands into the hot water and rinsed them. He followed suit. Behind his grotesque eagle mask, I could not tell whether he was enjoying this procedure or not. In any event, so far, so good. From my kit I took a clean linen towel, and wiped my hands, indicating that he should do likewise. It was only then that I turned my attention to the patient.

With the evidence of the chief's account, it seemed to me that a skull fracture was indicated, and so it proved. A swift examination of the boy's cranium showed that a sharp blow had indented the skull, breaking the bony structure and pressing a fragment in on the brain. It was not an uncommon accident in the annals of medicine, and in my studies I had read of cultures as far apart as ancient Grecians and South America Incas, who had developed their own methods of trephination, that is opening up the skull to relieve the pressure on the brain. But I had never had to cope with such a case myself.

The patient, as if in deep sleep, snored from time to time, due to the vibration of the paralyzed soft palate. In raising his eyelids I found the pupils dilated and fixed, signifying that the reflex to light was gone. Not an encouraging sign. His pulse was slow, but regular. Temperature high, but not dangerously so.

"Tell the chief — and the medicine man — that the head-bone is broken, and I — that is, we — must mend it."

Braithwaite passed on this information, which was received in silence.

"To do this," I went on, "we must shave part of the skull, bore a small hole, and lift the broken piece of bone up to its normal position."

The Indians listened closely as Braithwaite translated my words. The chief looked dubious, and turned to his medicine man, who responded by spreading his wings in this confined space, and glaring at me, hissing like a disturbed snake.

"Tell him," I said, at my wit's end, "tell the medicine man he can help to make a dead man come back to life, and be even more famous than he is now. With my modest assistance." Braithwaite seemingly translated this passage successfully, for the medicine fellow responded by peering first at me, then at the patient, and by cocking his head as if listening to the laboured snoring. Then he spoke to the chief.

"What does he say?" I asked.

"He says that he has been reading the thoughts of Shining Arrow, and he, Shining Arrow, approves of the operation. Thus the responsibility lies between Shining Arrow and yourself, doctor."

"Unless it is successful," I said, "in which case our medicine man will undoubtedly bask in glory. Rascal! I shall need more boiled water," I said. Braithwaite passed on my request to one of the squaws outside the tent.

I turned the young man's head to one side, and proceeded to clip the dark hair over the damaged part of the skull. Curiously there was no blood, dried or otherwise, the skin seemingly unperforated in the accident.

As the black locks came away, I handed them to the medicine man, who put them aside carefully, I assume for some future rite of his cultural heritage. So far, so good.

I took out my razor, and moistening the scalp with soap and water, I carefully shaved the critical area. The patient snored on. The chief watched with wise old eyes. The Eagle Man was alert, I think, for any theatrical devices which he could perhaps add to his own box of tricks.

Now, in a more critical stage of the operation, with a scalpel I incised a flap of the now naked skin, over the break in the bone, and I laid it back. A thin line of blood appeared. The chief rose to his feet in horror, and spoke to Braithwaite in a sharp undertone.

"What now?" I grunted.

"He thinks you're scalping his son," said Braithwaite.

"Tell him that I will put the scalp back, the boy will regain his senses, his hair will grow in again, and he will live to become a great chief of the tribe, and to honour his father."

Braithwaite spoke to Thunder Sky in quiet reassuring tones. Thus mollified, the old chief sat down again, watching my every move. It was well that he was reassured, for having located the break, I would now have to drill a small hole in the bone to adjust and secure the broken piece in its normal position. This I proceeded to do, with due care to disinfect the exposed parts and my instruments, according to good medical practice.

Before my drill bit into the skull of the unconscious youth, I glanced again at Thunder Sky, who sat alert, but without expression. I recalled hearing of sun dance ceremonies, in which young braves inserted strips of raw-hide under the skin of their chests, and leaned back with their full weight, facing the sun, until the raw-hide pulled out through skin and muscle. A mere hole in the skull would be child's play compared to that. Particularly since my patient, happily, was still quite unconscious.

The bit made its usual unpleasant sound as it drilled into the skull. Presently, careful not to touch the soft tissue, I removed the drill, and was able to get a grip with forceps to move the piece of bone to its proper position, and thus relieve the pressure on the brain. My patient at once stopped his unnatural snoring, and breathed more normally.

There was little to do now but to restore the scalp by sewing it back in place, which was quickly accomplished. The break in the skull, now in its normal position, would repair itself. Such is the wonder of nature.

I checked the patient's eyes. The retinas were now normal size, though still unfocussed. His pulse was normal, his breathing regular and deep. I bandaged the scalp and turned aside to tidy up my paraphernalia. I was aware of a sudden intake of breath from Chief Thunder Sky. I turned to him to see what troubled him, and saw that his eyes were fixed in wonder upon the face of his son. Following his gaze, my own heart gave a leap, for the boy's eyes were open, looking out calmly and with intelligence upon the world.

The medicine man was not long in responding. From the floor he snatched up a rattle. Crouching, he waved it two or three times over the recumbent figure on the bunk before diving headlong out of the teepee entrance, from where he rushed into the crowd, flapping his wings, and triumphantly crying aloud, like a veritable eagle itself. His cry was taken up by the entire community, and drums were heard pounding out a triumphal rhythm.

In the teepee, Thunder Sky had turned to me, his eyes glistening. I knew nothing of the nature of the North American Indian, though I had heard of stoical customs, such as the previously mentioned sun dance. All I know is, he reached forward to me, and embraced me with that most universal gesture of human affection. Then he took an eagle feather from his head, and laid it formally across my two hands, murmuring some words in his obscure language.

"What does he say?" I asked Braithwaite.

"He adopts you," said Braithwaite. "He welcomes you into his family as White Medicine. You must thank him, and give him some sort of gift in return."

Around my neck hung the stethoscope I had used in monitoring Shining Arrow's heart. On an impulse, I removed it and hung it around the neck of Thunder Sky, where it hung beside his golden necklace.

"Tell him he honours me with his welcome."

Braithwaite rattled off a few words and to my amazement, Thunder Sky then took his necklace of pure gold, and lifting it above his head, made a further incantation, and hung it around my neck, where it hung heavily. I was aware of Zachary's wide and envious gaze.

"Tell him this is too much," I said. Braithwaite responded with what sounded like a grand speech in the Indian tongue, and Zachary snarled angrily in my ear.

"What d'ya mean 'too much,'" he cried. "These people are knee deep in gold! That's why we're here!"

"I am here in answer to a plea to save a human life," I said.

"An Indian isn't human!" said Zachary. "Think I'd take all this trouble to save an Indian?"

"Why then?" I kept my temper under control.

"It's hangin' around your neck, Doc!" His voice rose in exasperation at my apparent density. "The whole tribe wears it like glass beads. It's gold, Doc. Gold!"

Outside, the tribal drums had reached a crescendo with the shouts and cries of the populace. Now they stopped suddenly, and within the tent, the old chief responded by pulling around his shoulder an ornately decorated ceremonial mantle. He dismissed Braithwaite and beckoned to me. I helped him to his feet. He moved to the door and went out. I followed, with Zachary and Braithwaite following close behind. Outside, the throng of Indians waited silently for confirmation of the words of the medicine man, who hopped towards us in his eagle regalia, flapping his wings, and creating raucous sounds. Thunder Sky lifted his hands, and with a surprisingly strong and resonant tone of voice he addressed the tribe.

Braithwaite translated the speech in an undertone. "He says that the life of his noble son, Shining Arrow, the greatest of the hunters, the bravest and most intelligent of the tribe, their future chief, has been saved by the skill and knowledge of Beaver Skin White Medicine. That's you, doctor, and that ratty old hat you have on." I straightened my moth-eaten piece of headgear. "He says that you were brought here from the world beyond the mountain, because of the love that is borne the Indians by Black Bonnet — that is Zachary — and Little Teacher — that's me, apparently. And we are to be honored. We can stay here as long as we please, or we can be escorted back to the trail out as soon as we wish. And in celebration there is to be a buffalo hunt tomorrow, to which we are invited."

"Buffalo hunt?" I queried.

"That's what he said."

"I thought the buffalo had vanished."

"From the prairies. But seemingly not from some of these remote valleys."

Formalities over, the crowd broke up, and went about their own business. We were escorted to a teepee which had been prepared for us. Our horses had been unloaded, and our personal gear and supplies were arranged neatly inside.

Before I settled down, I took Braithwaite to check on my patient. To my delight, he was conscious, and was being tended by two pretty young women, who were feeding him some kind of broth. They smiled shyly at us as we entered the teepee.

Braithwaite spoke softly to Shining Arrow, who replied, a puzzled expression on his face. The girls entered the conversation in quiet, soothing tones, and presently the patient relaxed. His eyes closed, and he slept.

"What was that about?" I asked.

"He was curious about what had happened to him. I think he is reassured."

I took the patient's pulse, and felt his forehead: both heart and temperature were normal. I nodded to my companion, and we withdrew, leaving the young warrior to his pretty young attendants.

As we returned to our tent, we could smell the air full of fragrant odours. Cooking fires flared around roasting venison. Salmon, fully three feet in length, split open from head to tail and sprinkled with herbs, sizzled before the flames. I realized how hungry I was.

In our teepee, Zachary was cleaning his Winchester. He had half a tumbler of whisky.

"Have you guys got your guns ready for tomorrow?" he asked with a grin.

"Guns?"

"Buffalo hunt."

"I hadn't thought of it."

"You've noticed these people haven't advanced beyond the stone age. They still use bows and arrows."

"Yes, I suppose so," I replied.

Zachary lifted his tumbler. "No booze," he said.

It was only then that I began to realize that indeed, the so-called rewards of civilization had so far passed by this remote mountain valley. At a time when the onrush of science and modern technology provided a railroad to span a continent, and guns to decimate the buffalo, these people lived self-contained lives, untouched by the outside world.

"Do they need guns?" I asked.

"I'll give them a demonstration tomorrow," replied Zachary.

"Or whisky?"

"See how it goes," he said with his malicious grin.

CHAPTER SEVEN

The Eagles Speak

I awoke as the sun's first rays touched the mountain peaks. Was it the light, or was it a sound that had awakened me. It came again. A thin cry — of Indian song, a single voice, uplifted in praise of a new day. My companions were asleep. I pushed aside my sleeping bag, and went out of the teepee.

The Indian community was not yet awake. Only a single brave sat cross-legged on the ground, facing the light of dawn. In his hand was a small song-drum, which he thumped softly from time to time. He was singing quietly, intimately almost, to an object I had failed to observe the previous day. He sat within a circle of white stones, and at their centre, on a short pole which brought it up to the level of his eyes, was the skull of a buffalo. Bleached white, with lowering horns, and dark eye-sockets, it seemed to listen silently to the quiet supplication of the Indian. Between the singer and the totem burnt a fire of a few twigs, barely noticeable in the growing light of morning.

Laying aside his drum, from a pouch embroidered with porcupine quills the singer took some grey powder in his fingers. He tossed the powder into the flames of the fire, his voice rising. A cloud of aromatic smoke ascended from the fire, and the rays of the rising sun came through a cleft in the mountain at this moment, illuminating the face of the singer. It was Chief Thunder Sky. I felt as if I were witnessing an ancient and sacred communion.

Then the moment was broken. Zachary emerged from the teepee. He was lighting one of his cheroots, approaching me in the dawn light.

He saw the old man conducting his quiet ceremony, and listened for a moment.

"He's prayin' for a good hunt," said Zachary. "Beggin' the buffalo's pardon. He'll just take what he needs for the tribe, he says. Something like that." He turned aside, not at all touched by the significance of the scene. "I'm hungry," he said. "Where's breakfast?" The camp was stirring, cooking fires were coming to life. "More venison, I guess," said Zachary.

"That doesn't sound unreasonable to me," I said.

"What, venison?"

"No. Just take what you need, and be thankful for it."

Zachary looked at me with suspicion. "What are you, Doc? A preacher or sump'n?" He chewed on his cigar angrily, and went back into the teepee.

Presently we had the first meal of the day, and as the sun rose in the sky, the excitement mounted. Young men on horseback, both horse and rider painted and decorated with feathers, swooped into the camp in a state of excitement. They spoke to the Eagle Man.

"Buffalo? What are they sayin' about buffalo?" cried Zachary.

"They've been scouting the buffalo since before dawn," said Braithwaite. "There is a herd grazing in a valley a few miles to the west."

"Let's git goin' then," retorted Zachary impatiently.

Then the Eagle Man did a curious thing. Ascending a nearby rocky pinnacle, he flapped his wings, and cried aloud to the empty sky. His hands, emerging from his feathers, clutched a rabbit which kicked frantically in his grasp. After a moment, two bald eagles appeared in the sky above, whereupon the Eagle Man tore off the head of the rabbit with his teeth, and held up the poor quivering thing high above him, the head in one hand, the body in the other. The eagles paused for a moment, seeming to hang in mid air, their forbidding eyes surveying the scene. Then, with a sudden movement of their great pinions, they dove down with alarming speed, the air whistling through their wings and tail feathers, talons reaching for a portion of the dismembered rabbit. In a moment, they had grasped the proffered gift, and with a great beat of wings, lifted off again into the sky.

The medicine man turned to the assembled company with bloody hands, and cried out over our heads. The crowd shouted its enthusiastic response.

Zachary, listening, turned pale. "What nonsense is this?" he snarled.

"What's the matter? What did he say?" I cried.

Braithwaite looked puzzled. "Something like good hunting," he said. "The eagles said so."

"Hunting of what?" said Zachary, uncomfortably.

"It was ambiguous," replied Braithwaite. "Either 'buffalo' or 'strangers'."

"A curious thing to say," I observed.

"He was lookin' at us when he said it," growled Zachary.

We did not have further opportunity to discuss the matter, because the assembled company turned towards us cheerfully enough, a young brave with his face painted vermilion and yellow vigorously addressing Braithwaite with gestures to the horses and to the horizon.

"He says we are invited to join the hunt, with whatever weapons we have, or just for the excitement. It's a great event."

"I've got my revolver," I said.

"I've got a rifle," said Braithwaite.

"And me, my Winchester," grunted Zachary. "We'll see who hunts who."

Before we were able to leave the encampment, Braithwaite and I took a moment to visit our patient. Inside the teepee, Shining Arrow was sitting up, wrapped in a deerskin cloak. His father, Thunder Sky, was with him. They both greeted us with ceremony: friendly enough, but with a certain dignified detachment. I felt the boy's pulse, took his temperature and so on, and all seemed to be well.

Braithwaite conversed with the old man. "He asks where Zachary is. I told him he is cleaning his gun for the hunt," said Braithwaite. The old man made a grimace, and spat out some words in anger. "Zachary has been here before, with his guns, he says. He is a bad man."

"Here before?" I asked. "On his own?"

"With two other white men. They debauched women, and took gold. They left disease."

I fingered the nugget at my throat. The motion caught the eye of the old chief. He spoke again and Braithwaite translated.

"White men kill each other for gold," he said. "But Zachary also brought White Medicine who saved the life of Shining Arrow, so what does Thunder Sky do? Does he kill Zachary because he is evil? Or does he reward him for bringing life to his son?"

I thought of the Eagle medicine man. In spite of myself, I had been impressed by his behaviour. He had a certain wisdom, it seemed to me, beyond the understanding of the contemporary European medical mind.

"What does the medicine man say?" I asked.

Braithwaite put the question to the old man, who replied in measured tones. "The eagles tell him that the hunter is hunted."

CHAPTER EIGHT

The Hunter Is Hunted

From accounts I had heard, I had some idea of the hundreds of thousands of bison which had roamed the western plains of North America, and which had provided the basis of a contained economy for the many tribes of plains Indians since time immemorial. I had also heard of the devastation wrought by the white buffalo hunters, and indeed by the Indians themselves in recent years, when fashionable European taste offered premium prices for the delicacy of buffalo tongues. Not infrequently, I had heard, beasts would be killed, the tongues alone would be taken, and the carcasses left to rot in the prairie sun. One buffalo hunter of Kansas, Thomas Linton by name, was proud of his record, claiming to have killed, single-handedly, more than three thousand beasts in one season.

In a few short years, this kind of excess virtually eliminated those noble animals from the plains, and the Indians of the region were driven to dependence upon the white economy.

This ran through my mind as Zachary, Braithwaite and I mounted our horses, and joined the young braves of this mountain tribe. Their dark skin gleaming with white, red and yellow pigment, eagle feathers in their hair, bows and quivers of arrows on their tawny backs, they exuded a palpable sense of excitement and anticipation. Straddling their barebacked mounts, they wheeled and galloped and checked the

The buffalo hunt

swift passage of their steeds, as if, like the centaur of old, the rider was one with his mount.

Presently, without a noticeably imposed order, the entourage streamed out of the camp, to the westward. There were no shouted commands or any obvious course of instruction, yet all moved in order, scouts ahead, older men behind, the impatient younger braves strung out, it seemed to me, like those patterns of wild geese one sees flying over the northern Canadian wilderness.

Within the V of this formation, a privileged position in company with the Eagle Man, rode Zachary, Braithwaite and myself. In their saddle holsters, Zachary and Braithwaite carried modern Winchester repeater rifles. I had only my army revolver, relic of the Afghan frontier, and a few rounds of ammunition. I was uncertain whether in fact I was up to deliberately shooting one of the beasts we were pursuing. I suppose, on reflection, that it was little different from the fashionable grouse shoot that I had occasionally attended in England, in which beaters were employed to beat the woods and drive the game birds towards the hunters, who, seated comfortably on their shooting sticks, could blaze way to their heart's content.

Certainly, in the present instance, one's heart beat faster, and one's responses were sharper than usual, the colours of the landscape and of the sky, and the omnipresent mountains more clearly defined. Thoughts coming one upon another, I wondered how my dear Holmes would have responded to this adventure. In all our years of acquaintance I had never seen him on a horse, though I would judge that his travel in foreign lands would on occasion demand a certain degree of horsemanship, in which, I have no doubt, he would excel, as he does with most skills he undertakes. Such aptitude as I possess I acquired, as I have said, in the Indian army, in mountainous country, in contact with ruthless Pathan tribes: not very unlike the situation in which I presently found myself. But at least, in the present circumstances, I was a guest of the natives, rather than a usurper, and looking around at the painted savages among whom I rode, I was grateful for that.

The sunlit glade through which we rode was carpetted with flowers. Wild birds flew up at our approach, partridge and the like. The air was buoyant and spring-like.

"This valley is quite like paradise," exclaimed young Braithwaite, as he rode up alongside me.

"I was thinking the same thing," I replied. "Untouched. Undefiled."

"Aren't those hot springs ahead of us?" he pointed. To one side a plume of steam issued from the rock, and clouded the surface of a series of small ponds, which lay sparkling in the sunlight.

"Sulphuric. More than one. They probably raise the temperature in this valley."

"I've not experienced that before," I said.

Zachary saw us in conversation, and hailed us. "Ready for the hunt, boys?" he shouted. His hat was pulled over his brow, the cord tied under his chin, presumably to prevent it blowing off in the chase. He squinted against the sun, grimacing the while.

He pulled his Winchester from its sheath. "When it comes to killin' buffalo," he cried, I guess we can show these savages a thing or two!" He laughed aloud. "Killin' anything else too, if it comes to it!"

Passing the hot springs, the entourage broke into a gallop. My cow-pony leaped ahead eagerly, and I clutched the pommel, keeping my seat in the saddle without too much difficulty. The Eagle medicine man was riding bareback. I wondered to what degree the wings and head-dress had become part of his personality, for he still wore them, mounted as he was on his galloping horse, the wings folded back out of the passage of the wind.

Presently the valley opened onto a rolling plain, which stretched back into the mountains, ringed by those stately, snow-shrouded peaks, and there, perhaps a mile distant, I perceived the herd of buffalo, perhaps two hundred head, grazing on the lush grass. Never before had I actually seen these beasts, and I felt a tingling of the scalp, and an increase in my pulse, a response, no doubt, as ancient as man's need to practise the hunt for his own survival.

I then saw that a small advance guard of some three or four young Indian warriors had advanced by a circuitous route well ahead of the main party; now, as we moved towards the herd, these young fellows, galloping at a furious pace, with loud cries and whistles, succeeded in stampeding the herd towards us. Our V formation had opened up, and as the buffalo rushed into it, a shower of lethal arrows cut them down. As they endeavoured to turn, some were trampled by their fellows, and our braves were in among the maddened beasts, discharging arrows with remarkable swiftness and accuracy. The horses themselves seemed to have a particular ability to avoid the plunging bodies of the great wild eyed creatures, and freed their lithe riders to shoot their arrows true to the mark.

More than once in the midst of the melee, much to my concern, I found my gammy leg pressed between the body of my horse and that of a plunging, fear-maddened buffalo, whose distended bloodshot eyeballs seemed to roll in its head, scarce a hand's breadth distant from my own, and foam from his fiery nostrils bespattered the leg of my trowsers. Yet I had no will to fire my revolver at the beast.

I had read accounts of British nobility setting up so-called "hunting parties" in the Canadian West, at great expense, bringing fancy carriages and exotic food, caviar, champagne, and the like, shooting everything they could lay their gun-sights on, in the name of sport. I have never been able to understand this strange urge, though in the present instance, the hunters were filling the larder for their own existence, conducting ceremonies to the Great Spirit, expressing their thanks.

... in the midst of the melee ...

Among the plunging bodies, the snorting animals, the blood, the thump of arrows finding their mark, I was also aware of the repeated crack from Zachary's rifle, as on his plunging steed he brought down as many buffalo as he might aim at. I caught a glimpse of him, black hat clamped on his head, cheroot between his teeth, in a sort of ecstasy of battle. Unlike the Afghan wars, where I had last ridden a horse amid gunfire and carnage, the enemy in this case did not fire back. It was, in fact, an unequal contest, and having brought down as many buffalo as the Indians felt they needed, a cry went up, the flight of arrows ceased, and the remainder of the buffalo herd lumbered away towards the distant mountains, leaving the Indians jubilant with the success of their venture.

Then I saw that Zachary, not content with the cease-fire, was still in the midst of the galloping herd, still bringing down plunging animals with his Winchester. Close behind him followed the Eagle medicine man, who was now standing erect on the undulating back of his galloping horse.

As I watched with astonishment, The Eagle Man uttered a screech like that of his totem brethren, and spreading his wings to a remarkable extent, launched himself into the air above the horse; retaining control of the reins with his feet, he was drawn along by his galloping mount, the updraft on his great spread wings sufficient to support him in mid-air. Thus engaged, the medicine man called again his imperious eagle cry, and as if in response, there was a sudden pulsating rush of air from the sky, the beating of great wings, and over the plunging bodies of the retreating buffalo, and of Zachary, descended a flock of eagles, perhaps six in number, swooping and gliding, fierce of eye, claws extended, beaks ready to strike.

Again the medicine man cried aloud, his eagle voice sounding sharp and clear above the rumble of galloping hooves, the crack of Zachary's rifle, and the swish of eagle wings. At the cry, the voracious birds fell upon Zachary's dark figure, and through the beat of giant wings, I saw his arms go vainly above his head to beat back his attackers. He stood up in his stirrups and flailed the air with his rifle, his horse galloping freely under him in company with the stampeding bison. In a moment it was over. Under the onslaught of the great birds, Zachary fell from his saddle, and was lost under the pounding hooves of the buffalo herd. Curved beaks dripping blood, the eagles rose in the air in serene flight, and were gone.

The medicine man reined in his mount, and was once more astride his horse's back, solemnly folding his great wings. This done, he wheeled and trotted back, making his way through the strewn bodies of the fallen animals. Young braves had already dismounted, and were administering the *coup de grâce* to the many wounded creatures.

Braithwaite had joined me, flushed with the chase. It was only then that I was aware of two figures bringing up the rear of the party, astride the bare backs of their horses. They sat almost regally, in garb of embroidered deerskin, eagle plumes in their hair, their faces devoid of paint. One was the old Chief Thunder Sky. The other, my bandage around his dark head, was his noble son, Shining Arrow. Thunder Sky held an ancient stone tomahawk in his hand, an emblem, I assumed, of his authority. He held it aloft as he approached us.

The medicine man stopped before the pair and made them a formal salutation before exchanging a few words with the chief. He then departed quietly in the direction of the settlement. Thunder Sky then turned his attention to Braithwaite and myself.

He spoke in ringing tones. Braithwaite translated his words. "The evil hunter has been hunted. The slayer has been slain. Justice has been done."

The chief and his son turned their mounts, and quietly retraced their course to the encampment.

CHAPTER NINE

The Lost World

It was the following day. Every able member of the community was involved in cutting up the buffalo, and preparing meat and hides for future use. With Braithwaite I checked my patient for the last time. The young man's condition was much improved, and we wished him and the chief well, before mounting our horses. Thunder Sky accompanied us to the rocky defile which led from the lush valley to the outside world. Before us the land rose precipitously in crags and ledges reaching to the cloud-capped snow fields and mountain tops. I noticed that more than one young brave was perched on the ragged rocks above the defile, but I paid little attention.

Presently we came to the narrow gully through which we had entered some days ago, and Thunder Sky stopped and raised his stone tomahawk in a final salute. We left the noble chief there, and in a few minutes, the roar of the falls echoing ever louder in our ears, we went through the tunnel-like defile leading to the outer world. There was a sudden drenching downfall of glistening water and we passed through it to emerge into the familiar rock-strewn valley beyond.

A moment later I became conscious of a dull rumble that shook the earth upon which we stood. It continued for fully a minute or so, before subsiding.

"What in God's name was that?" I said to my companion. We had stopped the horses, and the skeletal tree stretched its bare and ragged branches across the bank of the river. A moment passed.

"I don't know," he said. "Perhaps we might go back and look."

I agreed, and we retraced our steps. A short distance behind the falls, the narrow gully through which we had just come was now quite impassable, filled with new-fallen stone and great boulders, the like of which I had seen above us in the narrow defile, perched on the mountainside only a few minutes before.

We returned through the waterfall, and turning a corner in the trail found ourselves face to face with Sherlock Holmes and Superintendent Steele, in company with two N.W.M.P. constables.

"Hullo, Watson," said Holmes. "You look a bit damp."

"Yes, I am a bit," I responded.

A constable was just taking a blackened pot off a small fire. The party was taking its ease.

"Lost Zachary, did you?" Superintendent looked us over.

Braithwaite and I exchanged glances. "In a manner of speaking, sir," he replied.

"What kind of a response is that, Constable Braithwaite?" said Steele, with some asperity. "Did you, or did you not, lose the man?"

"Yes sir, I did. He is dead. Quite dead. Trampled to death under a stampede of buffalo."

It was Steele's and Holmes' turn to exchange glances. "Buffalo?" queried Steele.

"Yes, sir. Buffalo," responded Braithwaite. "Hundreds of buffalo. In the Headless Valley, beyond the falls."

The superintendent looked at Braithwaite, and chewed his great mustache. Holmes fished in his capacious coat pocket for his briar pipe, which he commenced to fill.

"Constable Braithwaite," said Superintendent Steele at length. "Perhaps you had better get down off your horse, stand by the fire to dry off, have a cup of tea and make me a verbal account of your affairs to date, before you submit an official report."

"Very good, sir," said Braithwaite, and he obediently dismounted. I followed his example.

Holmes blew out a cloud of fragrant tobacco smoke which rose and mingled with branches of the pine trees. Beyond the trees, the mighty mountains maintained their watch.

"At the foot of the falls, Watson," said Holmes, "on the far side of the river, we found two skeletons. Their heads were missing."

"Oh?" I shivered, the result, no doubt, of the double shower I'd had in the waterfall. I moved closer to the fire, and gratefully accepted a mug of hot tea from a constable.

"There were rusty picks and shovels," Holmes went on. "Half-buried in debris washed down by the stream. We also found two or three small raw-hide sacks, carrying the figure of a porcupine. The sacks were empty."

"I see," I replied.

From the wilderness of the lonely mountain came a vagrant wind, moaning in and swaying the great pine trees above our heads. A chill ran through me, despite the heat from the fire and the cup of hot tea in my hands.

"You heard the landslide, Holmes, a few minutes ago," I said.

"Landslide?" said Holmes.

"Yes. A dull rumble that shook the ground. You must have noticed it."

"No." He looked at me askance.

I gesticulated with my cup of tea. "Where we've been, Holmes, we found a land ringed with mountains."

"Yes?"

"It is beautiful beyond description. Lush grass and flowers, streams of warm water springing out of the rock. There are herds of buffalo, and happy people untouched by the outside world. The place is like the Garden of Eden."

"Really, Watson," Holmes sounded almost embarrassed, his tone one of disbelief.

"Lost forever. The road to it is now impassable," I said.

The cold wind came again, and with it a swirling gust of snow. I pulled my sheepskin around me. The sun had disappeared.

3

The Lady
of the Camellias

Our train stopped at a way station, where the great panting engine was supplied with water for the arduous haul through the heart of the Rocky Mountains. A few passengers came on board during the pause. A pair of lithe, brown-skinned Indians put a slender birchbark canoe in the baggage-car, along with a bundle or two, before they climbed on board the carriage ahead of us. A heavyset man in a loud checked suit presented a ticket to the porter on the platform, and was allowed admittance to our carriage.

Holmes and I, after paying our respects to the Western representative of the North West Mounted Police, the famed Superintendent Steele in Calgary, had boarded the train with a view to visiting Canada's West coast, at the invitation of Sir Matthew Begbie, the extraordinary individual whom Queen Victoria appointed to bring law and order to British Columbia during those turbulent days of the gold rush at Barker Creek. It had been a time when thousands of "rough-necks" spilled over from the depleted fields of the California Gold Rush of the early 1890s, and had flowed unrestricted into Canada, lured by the tales of gold in the Cariboo.

At the time, officers of law and order in Canada had not yet assumed authority in British Columbia, and the railway had not yet gone through. There were murmurs from the American government that if Canada could not police the region effectively, then perhaps America should annex it, and so look after the interest and safety of its citizens. In response to this, Queen Victoria invested the powers of life and death in the region to one Matthew Begbie, a six foot two inch gentleman who played the lute and sang Italian opera in his leisure moments. Although he did have legal training, "I know little of law, but everything of justice," Begbie is reported as saying, and within months of his appointment, the "Hanging Judge" as he came to be called, riding his great black stallion over the mountain trails of British Columbia, imposed his form of justice on the Cariboo Gold Fields, and was respected by roughneck and cheechako alike. Under Begbie's surveillance, some millions of dollars worth of gold moved safely down the Cariboo Road from the gold fields to Vancouver, San Francisco and the world markets, and America did not find it necessary to intervene. Begbie had been knighted for his efforts, and had retired on Vancouver Island.

Holmes looked up from the paper he was reading. The heavyset man in the loud suit had taken a vacant seat in the further end of the carriage, in front of us. He carried a canvas bag, which thumped heavily as he set it between his legs on the floor of the carriage. His clothes looked brand new. His hand came up to take off his hat, disclosing a head of closely cropped hair.

"A member of a chain gang not long ago, recently released from an American penitentiary," murmured Holmes.

"Chain gang?" I said quietly.

"The mark of irons on his wrist. His release so recent, his hair is not yet grown in. A brand new suit, not inexpensive. From the sound and apparent weight of his bag, he carries a heavy metal object in it."

At the stop, newspapers had come on board, and a ragged urchin was distributing them.

"Paper, sir?" he asked.

"Give me one please," said Holmes, handing over a coin, never satisfied unless he could read the police news and the agony column. "And can you take a collect telegram to the station for me, my fine young fellow?" Holmes was already scribbling a few words on the back of an envelope. He folded it over. "And that's for your trouble," he said, taking a fifty cent piece from his pocket and handing both envelope and coin into the boy's grubby hand. "See it gets off, will you?"

"Right away, sir," said the urchin, and he went away on his mission, imbued with self-importance.

There was much puffing from the locomotive, and in a few moments, with much grinding of wheels, the train was again in motion.

"Sarah Bernhardt captivates Canada," said Holmes.

"What?" I replied.

"Newspaper heading. *The Lady of the Camellias, Sarah Bernhardt on a tour which has carried her with triumph over half of America,"* said Holmes. "New York, Boston, Florida, San Francisco. She's now about to appear in Vancouver." He handed me the front page of the paper.

"The Great Bernhardt!" I exclaimed, in sudden excitement. "I say, Holmes, we are on our way to Vancouver. I do trust we can get tickets to see her perform."

"Oh, do you?" Holmes glanced at me, amused apparently at my enthusiasm.

"She is a fascinating woman, Holmes," I expostulated, "and an utterly captivating actress. The greatest of her time. I saw her once in Paris."

"A bit eccentric, is she not?" said Holmes, and he turned again to the agony column.

"Genius like hers is allowed its eccentricity," I responded. I looked at the newspaper. "Just listen to this, would you?" I cried. *"Madame Bernhardt's triumph was her matinee performance of* La Dame aux Camélias. *There were seventeen curtain calls after the third act, and twenty-nine at the finish. Upon her attempted exit from the theatre, she was literally mobbed, chiefly by hysterical women trying to speak to her, to shake her hand, to touch her. One overwrought girl held out an autograph book, and when she realized she had brought no ink, bit into her own wrist, and dipped the pen in blood!"*

"Exactly," said Holmes. "Excessive." He was deep in the agony column, seemingly more to his taste than the account of the finest actress in the world. I dropped the paper to expostulate, and I froze in horror, for there, peering over the folded page, was a black snake! It had eyes like diamonds, and a forked tongue that darted in and out of its pink mouth.

I glanced at Holmes. He was still immersed in his reading. "I say, Holmes," I said.

"What, old chap?" He did not raise his eyes.

"Is that not a snake?"

"A snake!" He looked up alertly. "Good Lord, Watson, it is a snake!" Without hesitation, and with a swift movement, Holmes reached out his right hand, and between finger and thumb, grasped the creature firmly behind the head. He lifted it up and peered at it with great interest. It was fully three feet in length.

"A fine specimen of Dipsadine. From the swampy Everglades of Florida, if I am not mistaken." The snake flicked its little tongue in Holmes' direction, and bared its tiny fangs.

"Hullo," Holmes looked up. "Here is the owner, I have no doubt."

The door to the adjoining railway carriage had opened, and a slender, theatrical-looking fellow entered. He appeared flushed and concerned, his clothing in disarray as he peered under seats and passengers' hand-baggage.

"Hullo there," Holmes raised his voice above the rumble of the train. He held the snake up to full view. "Is this what you are looking for?"

Our fellow passengers, attention attracted by Holmes' voice, looked blank for the most part, their eyes first looking at the creature writhing in Holmes' grip, and then moving to take in the response from the new arrival in the carriage. The latter, seeing the reptile safely in Holmes' hands, came quickly forward. He repressed a shudder.

"I hate snakes," he said. "I cannot bear to touch them."

"And yet you were searching for it, were you not?" asked Holmes.

"I have been made responsible for the confounded creature."

"Then to whom does the reptile belong?" queried Holmes. The snake had coiled itself with apparent comfort around his arm.

"Madame Bernhardt acquired it in Florida," replied our visitor.

"Madame Bernhardt?" said Holmes.

"Yes. She has a confounded alligator in there too. As well as other beasts." He gestured in the direction of the carriage from which he had just come, his carefully coifed hair in disarray, his brow moist with perspiration.

"Sarah Bernhardt on this train?" I cried.

"Yes. We have the last five carriages." The fellow mopped his brow with a handkerchief which smelled of violets. "She has four carriages to carry the company on tour. The last is her own. She is an efficient manager, you know, as well as a great actress. And a collector."

"Collector?" I queried.

"Oh yes," I thought his voice a little petulant. "Animals, jewelry, statuary, snakes, men. Anything, anybody, that strikes her fancy. It was her fancy that diverted us through the Canadian Rocky Mountains, presumably for the excitement." It was apparent that he did not share the lady's view.

"We play in Vancouver tomorrow. *La Dame aux Camélias.*"

"What are we to do with this creature, then?" queried Holmes, coming back to the point at hand. "Will you take it back to Madame Bernhardt with our compliments?" He offered the reptile to the fellow, who recoiled in dismay.

"I can't touch the beast!" he exclaimed.

"Well then," said Holmes after a moment. He glanced at me with devilment in his eye. "Perhaps we could take it to the lady ourselves."

I looked at Holmes in wonder. To meet Madame Sarah Bernhardt in person was quite beyond my imagination. She was literally the toast of the civilized world. Duels had been fought over her, her slightest whim indulged by the rulers of more than one country. Our own "Bertie," Prince of Wales, heir to the throne of England, had gone on bended knee to kiss her hand, paying tribute to her unique talent and captivating personality.

The young man seemed greatly relieved at Holmes' suggestion. "Would you?" he exclaimed. "I'm sure Madame Bernhardt would be most grateful. And so should I," he added, repressing a delicate shudder.

"Come along, Watson," cried Holmes, and started down the aisle. The snake was now coiled around his neck, apparently fast asleep.

"Mr. Watson, is it?" queried our guide.

"Doctor, actually," I replied.

"Ah! And you, sir?" He glanced at Holmes.

"Holmes," said Sherlock Holmes. "Mister."

"Good. Thank you so much, gentlemen. One must know where one is, speaking with Madame Sarah."

So saying, he opened the connecting door to the next carriage, and led the way through. As he did so, I wondered how the snake had managed to pass unaided from one carriage to another. But I had little time to solve that problem, as we proceeded through three Pullman cars in which members of Madame Sarah's cast rehearsed lines for the

The fabulous Sarah Bernhardt ...

evening performance, played solitaire, slept, or otherwise passed the time.

The fourth car was a dining room, with a formal table for ten set up the length of it, and a kitchen wherein I glimpsed male cooks at work, preparing what smelled like excellent French cuisine. Wine bottles rattled on racks over their heads. We moved into the fifth car. A subtle perfume hung in the air. Underfoot were lustrous Persian carpets and zebra skins. The windows of the carriage were draped with some silken fabric which was caught up in swags with heavy tassels.

There were divans, and easy chairs, a reading table covered with French and English magazines, a writing table, an upright piano, card tables, a number of potted plants, and a profusion of flowers. Under one of the tables lay an alligator, fully three feet in length, which I would have thought to be a stuffed specimen had it not chosen that moment to yawn, disclosing a formidable array of teeth.

A silk screen concealed part of the carriage. Venturing beyond it, I caught a glimpse of an immense brass bed, piled with many pillows. Among the pillows, the lithe form of a panther was stretched, a diamond-studded collar around its slender neck. So this was "The Palace Car," the travelling abode of the fabulous Sarah Bernhardt.

"'Alt!" An imperious female voice rang out. I stopped abruptly as the lady herself stepped out from behind the curtain. In her hand was a pearl-handled pistol, levelled directly at my head.

Our escort, who had been silent to this point, burst into a babble of French, gesticulating and seemingly guaranteeing our innocence and good intentions, and the return of Madame's pet snake. At this voluble outburst, Madame Sarah slowly lowered her pistol and regarded us solemnly. Then she gave us a brilliant and winning smile, and in a moment was a delicate and vulnerable female, towards whom one's protective instincts flowed.

"*Mille pardons, messieurs,*" her voice was warm and intimate. "I am a woman on my own, do you see, a stranger travelling zis wild western country. One mus' be prepared, *n'est-ce pas?*"

"Truly, madame," Holmes bowed, the snake now cradled in his arms. "You are wise, as well as singularly beautiful, if I may say so."

I looked at Holmes with surprise. He, notorious for his avoidance of the female sex, was behaving like a veritable courtier. Madame Sarah gave Holmes a calculating look, then directed her attention to the snake. She took the creature in her slender arms, making cooing noises. *"Merci, messieurs,* for your kindness. But I do not know your names."

"I am Sherlock Holmes, madame, and my companion is Doctor Watson."

"'Ow do you do, gentlemen. A glass of champagne, *peut-être?"* Without waiting for a reply, she had glided around the screen into the salon, and pulled on a slender bell-rope. In a moment, one of the stewards appeared. He must have anticipated Madame's thoughts, for on a silver tray he carried a bottle of Pol Roger 86, and three champagne glasses. He set the tray and its contents on one of the small tables. Madame nodded to him and to the young fellow who had led us into her boudoir, and they promptly disappeared, leaving us alone with the lady.

"Perhaps, Monsieur 'olmes, you would be good enough to open ze bottle, and pour ze wine?"

"It would give me pleasure, madame," said Holmes.

Bernhardt sat down upon a couch, caressing the snake. Her luminous eyes were watching Holmes. "You 'ave 'ands ver' slender, *m'sieur,* an' strong, I theenk. Ver' sensitive," she said, after a moment.

Although I have myself commented more than once on Holmes' hands, I had never thought such observations could be articulated so warmly, and so persuasively, and I felt a flush of jealousy that Holmes, who had previously shown so little apparent interest in Sarah Bernhardt, should now be the centre of her attention.

Under Holmes' expert fingers, the champagne cork popped out of the bottle, and with a flourish, he filled the glasses on the silver tray, and offered them to La Bernhardt and to me, before taking one himself.

"To your continued success and excellent health, Madame," cried Holmes. We raised our glasses.

"Thank you, *messieurs,"* replied the lady, with a captivating smile.

We drank our champagne. But in a moment the impetuous creature had risen to her feet, discarding the snake in the process. "But 'ere we are, *messieurs,* travelling through some of ze grandest mountain scenery in ze world, and we are seated h'inside."

She flung a chinchilla cape around her slender shoulders, and two or three flimsy silk scarves, which floated in the air with her every move. "Bring ze wine outside, *m'sieurs*. We will toast ze sublime countryside through which we travel. I find it most thrilling. Eet touches ze soul."

The carriage in which we found ourselves was, in fact, the last on the train, allowing La Bernhardt the privilege of having the observation platform for her own personal and private use. We followed her out onto the deck, the train rattling and swaying underfoot.

"You may wonder what I was doing, messieurs, zat I should have welcomed you with a pistol in my hand," said Madame Bernhardt, raising her lovely voice easily above the passage of the train.

"Not at all, madame," said Holmes, as if the incident were commonplace.

"I do not trust ze banking system, do you see, and I carry the company's finances with me. In gold."

"In gold, madame?"

"*Oui.* In an iron-bound trunk, under my bed." She nodded her lovely head in the direction of the be-cushioned brass bedstead, and its feline occupant. "At last count zere was two hundred and fifty thousand dollars in there, in gleaming gold coin." She tossed off her champagne, and I choked on mine, much to my embarrassment.

"My word!" exclaimed Holmes.

"After Vancouver, we return to New York for a final performance of *La Dame aux Camélias*. We will have given one hundred and fifty-one performances, eight different plays in fifty-one cities, and I will return to France, richer by about three hundred thousand dollars."

"In gold coin," said Holmes.

"In gold coin," said the lady.

"I presume you take safety measures, madame," I ventured.

In reply, Sarah Bernhardt handed Holmes her empty champagne glass. Then, in the next moment, she turned upon us with a lithe movement like a veritable panther, her silk scarves flying in the wind. In each hand, as if by magic, she held a Colt revolver. I recoiled in amazement.

"When I say 'Go,' gentlemen, be good enough to toss your glasses into ze air. Behind the tren," she added. "Ready? Go!"

Obediently, we threw our glasses in the air. Swift as summer lightning her slender hands moved, the revolvers fired, and the fragile champagne glasses were shattered in mid air, shards of glass falling on the railway ties as we sped on our way into the mountain vastness.

Madame Sarah put her guns away and smiled sweetly.

"Does zat answer your question, Doctor Watson?"

"Indeed it does, madame," I responded. I looked at Holmes. I had never seen such open admiration on his face.

"Gentlemen," announced the lady. "I am told that one of ze unusual delights of travelling by rail through the Rocky Mountains is to sit in front of ze engine itself, upon what I believe they call ze 'cow-catcher.' I understand that ze Governor General's wife and other eminent ladies have been thrilled by zat h'experience. The railway 'as been good enough to invite me to 'ave such an adventure, as we approach ze Kicking 'orse Pass, where ze curves of ze railway through ze mountains offer most spectacular views. I believe we are coming to zat section now. I would be most pleased, gentlemen, of your company in zis adventure."

"I would be most honored to accept," replied Holmes with a bow.

"I also," I said. "Most delighted, madame."

In a few minutes, steaming and clanking, the train drew to a stop, and an entourage of railway officials made their way down the side of the track to the back of the train, to enquire after Madame Sarah's health, and whether she still desired to ride on the engine. She replied enthusiastically that indeed she did, and she would like the company of these two charming gentlemen who had returned her pet snake.

The good railwaymen looked a little nonplussed at the reference to the snake, but agreed that the cow-catcher could accommodate three of us in safety, and so, like royalty, we were escorted the length of the train, and seen safely to our perches in front of the giant engine. In a few minutes the train was again underway, penetrating ever further into the most spectacular parts of the Rocky Mountains.

Presently, the ascent became so precipitous that the road-bed that had been blasted out of the mountain lay in successive gradual curving loops, so that looking back from our perch on the engine, we could see below us the track over which we had just travelled, gleaming in the sun. Suddenly it became dark as we rushed into a tunnel burrowed into the heart of the mountain. Then we burst out again into sunlight, to our relief and delight, as new vistas opened up, and our excellent train made its way through this incredible landscape.

What the experience meant to the heightened artistic awareness of Madame Sarah I can only guess. What I saw was her fabulous profile lifted in ecstasy against the onrush of the wind, her draperies flowing about her like the figurehead of some sea-going galleon breasting the ocean waves.

Watching her, I saw her attention shift. Her head came around, her eyes sharpened, and in a moment she was transformed. Years ago, from the back seats of a Paris theatre, I had had the breathtaking privilege of seeing Bernhardt's on-stage performance of *The Lady of the Camellias.* Now, perched precariously on a platform in front of a locomotive in the wilds of the Rocky Mountains, I was about to participate with her in one of the most dramatic scenes in my life.

As I watched, her ecstasy vanished, and in its place a tumultuous rage seized her. Her beautiful face became convulsed with anguish, and a scream escaped her mouth that challenged the steam whistle of the locomotive that drew us through the mountains. She stood up on her precarious perch in front of the engine, lifting her hands in imprecation, as if she would stop the train by main force. With a sweeping gesture, she pointed downward at an angle from her vantage point, and burst into a volley of French curses which would have made a longshoreman blush.

"Arrêtez!" she cried. "Stop thees tren! Zere 'as been a great tren robbery! My private carriage 'as gone!" She screamed and gesticulated, her white scarves billowing in the wind. Far below us on the curving track, rolling away from us down the grade, was Bernhardt's private car. Situated as it had been at the back of the train, it had obviously been uncoupled in our absence, and, thus freed, had rolled away down the gradient, propelled by the force of gravity.

I thought at once of the unprepossessing fellow who had boarded the train at the whistle stop, and of his heavy canvas bag.

Holmes took in the situation at a glance. He stood up on the cowcatcher. "Madame," he cried. "Give me your pistols."

The train was slowing to a stop, and worried engineers looked out from the engine to ascertain the problem.

"My pistols, *m'sieur?"* Bernhardt drew herself up grandly, as if to protect herself. "Are you be'ind zis outrage, *m'sieur?"*

"I would advise you to do as I recommend, madame," Holmes' voice was commanding.

"W'y should I?" The woman was adamant.

"To regain your hard-won quarter of a million dollars, madame." Holmes eyes were like steel. The grand lady's lustrous orbs met their challenge for a long moment. Then I swear she blushed, and inclined her graceful neck like a schoolgirl.

"*M'sieur,*" she said quietly, and without another word, handed over the two Colt revolvers.

"Come, Watson," cried Holmes, and scrambled off the engine onto the railway tracks. The train was already in reverse, preparing to loop its way back down the mountain side.

I could see Holmes' intention. It was to go straight down the precipitous slope, cutting across the curves of the railway lines, and thus intercept the runaway carriage, which of course, was obliged to follow the track.

Holmes plunged over the edge, and I followed, feeling as if I were once again on the Afghan frontier. To be flung into such a moment of danger I find inspiring. One's energy flows to the utmost, one's judgment and physical awareness are at their highest peak. Here a scree of broken rock which one slides down amidst dust and flying pieces of dislodged stone. There, the inclined face of rock from which one springs to the next level below. To undertake such an exercise in cold blood would be quite unthinkable, but when the game is afoot, as in battle, one rises above the purely physical into a state approaching ecstasy. So I was lifted on this tumultuous passage down the side of the mountain, in spite of my gammy leg.

We gained on the runaway carriage, crossing the railway lines twice as it looped down the mountainside. Below us the gleaming rails levelled out as they led into a tunnel. In a moment the fleeing carriage would enter the portal, slowing down in its passage.

"See there, Watson," said Holmes tersely, "where the car comes out of the tunnel. There is a vantage point from which we can jump on top of it. Are you game?"

"As ever, Holmes," I panted.

We scrambled down the bank, the tunnel beneath us echoing with approaching rumble of the runaway car. In a moment it reappeared, travelling at this point quite slowly with the change in gradient, thank heaven, for otherwise I'm sure that I at least would not have made it. As it was, Holmes made a cat-like jump, and as I followed him, crashing down like a load of coals, he was already poised on the coach roof to give me a steadying hand.

"Good man, Watson," he murmured appreciatively. "Observation platform," he said, and he led the way down the roof of the coach, feeling in his generous pockets for the Colt revolvers he had borrowed from Madame Sarah.

I followed Holmes as best I could. Reaching the end of the coach, I turned for a moment to look ahead the way we were going. I recoiled in horror. Perhaps half a mile down the track, the line diverted into a siding, and I could see, waiting for us, the figures of two or three mounted men.

"I say, Holmes," I cried. "We appear to have a welcoming committee."

"Yes, Watson, I have already seen them," replied my friend, with which he swung himself down onto Madame Sarah's erstwhile observation deck. I followed less boldly. Holmes opened the door to the carriage, and a most fiendish cry from within assailed my ears. In the Punjab I had the occasion to attend the odd tiger hunt, so I was not entirely unfamiliar with the fearsome cry of an angry feline. But to encounter such a sound in the close quarters of a speeding railway carriage on the side of the Rocky Mountains, was a situation I never thought to experience.

As I entered the carriage, a marvelous sight met my eye. Stubby legs clasped grimly around one of Madame Sarah's chandeliers, there was the fellow we had spotted entering our carriage at the whistle stop earlier in the day. In one hand he had a crow-bar which he swung at the panther when it ventured too close for comfort. The graceful animal had no trouble avoiding the swinging blows, and indeed, from the torn condition of the man's checked trowsers, the creature had more than once got under the fellow's guard.

"Git this wild animal offen me," bleated the rascal. "I can't hold on any longer."

"You should have thought of that before you undertook the job," said Holmes.

At our presence, the panther looked up amicably, and like a domestic cat, ceased its horrid yowling. In a moment it went to a bowl of milk, and was presently back on the voluptuous bed among the cushions where I had first seen it.

The bandit still clung to the chandelier. He peered about in some concern. "Where's the alligator?" he wanted to know.

I was getting nervous about the knot of men that I had glimpsed at little distance down the track. On the flat ground of the plateau, the carriage was slowing down. I glanced out the door, and directed my gaze beyond the observation platform.

"Holmes," I said. "They are switching us onto the siding."

Our prisoner slid down from his perch, a grin on his face. "You seen 'em, did ya? Pals of mine."

Holmes had produced Madame Sarah's revolvers, one of which he tossed to me. "See if he's armed, Watson."

Quickly I frisked our prisoner. "No firearms. A knife." I took away a wicked-looking blade.

"I don't need a gun, with my lot waiting fer me. We'll dump Madame Whatsername's gold into our saddlebags, and skedaddle back over the border. My pals've got guns, an' they'll shoot whoever gets in the way."

The wheels of the carriage rattled over the switching points. We had slowed virtually to a stop.

"Back to Pensacola Penitentiary, and the chain gang," said Holmes.

"Pensacola!" snarled the fellow." What does a limey like you know about that hellhole?" The cocky grin had vanished.

"Just by reputation," said Holmes. "I can hardly blame you for breaking out, if perhaps you had used the opportunity to mend your ways."

Out of the carriage window we could see the welcome committee waiting for us to roll to a standstill, a heavyset bearded man in a wolf-skin jacket, and a skinny one sporting a handlebar mustache. The latter put down the iron bar he had used to switch the railway track, and in its place, he now held a Winchester .303 rifle. Impatiently they stood there, their faces split in vacuous grins, awaiting the anticipated delivery of a quarter of a million dollars in gold coin. They had three horses with saddlebags, one presumably for our prisoner. The latter made as if to move, but Holmes stopped him with a motion of his pistol.

Our railway car stopped, and there was silence, broken only by the whinny of one of the horses.

"Where the hell's Joe?" The puzzled cry came from the thin fellow with the handlebar mustache. He called aloud. "Joe, hey, Joe!" His voice re-echoed across the rocky surface.

"He must be inside," said Wolfskin.

"Or fallen off the train," snickered Handlebar nervously.

"All the more for us," replied his companion. Still they made no move, and their horses shifted restlessly, their hooves sounding hollow on the rock.

In the carriage, our prisoner looked from Holmes to myself in quiet agony, a quarter of a million dollars within his grasp, horses and escort waiting for him to escape over the border, and Holmes and me standing in his way.

Outside, there was a click from Handlebar's rifle as he cocked the firing mechanism. "I'm goin' on board," he said to his companion. "Watch out fer me." He approached the observation platform, and started to climb up.

Holmes waited, then at a critical moment as the fellow was poised on the rail, he fired a shot from his pistol, striking the rifle, sending it flying out of the man's hands, and tumbling the startled fellow to the deck, where he sat rubbing his fingers and gaping with surprise.

The fellow on the ground reacted by hauling a rifle out of its saddle-holster, but Holmes, with another precise shot, struck it out of his hands. I had a momentary vision of Holmes in London, peppering the wall of our digs with pistol-shot, inscribing the letters "V.R." in the plaster.

Then there was a clatter of horses' hooves nearby, and out of a rocky defile emerged a young N.W.M.P. sergeant with two constables. Holmes stepped out on the observation deck to watch the police dismount.

"Hello there, Corporal," called Holmes.

The young corporal came forward and saluted. One of his men was already taking in charge the fellow in the wolfskin.

"Sherlock Holmes, sir?" cried the corporal.

"Yes, Corporal."

"Thank you for your tip, sir. All we need now is the ringleader. Broke away from the Pensacola chain gang. We have been on his trail for some days."

Inside the railway carriage, the voice of the young corporal came through clearly. I saw the fire go out of my prisoner. Through the door, Holmes nodded to me, and I escorted the man out, his shoulders bowed in defeat.

Climbing over the rail, he and Handlebar quietly gave themselves up to the police, who put handcuffs on them, and helped them onto their horses.

I was aware of the train coming slowly up the track behind us. There was a quiet bump as our observation car was reconnected.

The young corporal had mounted his horse and was about to move out. He called again to Holmes. "Superintendent Steele sends his compliments to you, sir, to Doctor Watson, and to the gorgeous Madame Sarah. That's his phrase, sir. He is sorry he cannot attend her performance in Vancouver. Perhaps next time." The smart young fellow saluted again, and, turning his horse, led the way along the narrow trail leading from the railway.

In Vancouver, Holmes and I discovered to our delight that the Royal Box of the new quarter million dollar theatre had been reserved for us. That evening, Madame Sarah's performance of *La Dame aux Camélias* was undoubtedly the most moving theatrical experience I have ever had. And as the final curtain fell, my friend Sherlock Holmes unashamedly wiped away a tear before he stood up to applaud.

4

Sherlock Holmes
and the King of Siam

CHAPTER ONE

Sir Matthew Begbie
and His Siamese Visitors

The splendid strains of a Royal Navy band greeted Holmes and me as we stepped from our carriage in front of Sir Matthew Begbie's residence on Vancouver Island. The stirring theme of "Hearts of Oak" was being played with a vigor that stirred the blood in one's veins.

We entered the grounds, and handsome figures swirled around us: young women dressed in chiffon finery of the latest fashion; gallant naval officers, the gold braid of their formal uniforms sparkling in the sunlight, gracing the formal occasion; older folk, the backbone of the thriving community, more sedate in dress and deportment, nevertheless bright of eye and appreciative of the occasion.

After our passage through the Rockies, the balmy air of the Pacific heralded the approach of spring, and Sir Matthew's gardens were a riot of burgeoning blossom and the promise of summer.

It seemed to be a Naval occasion, and impeccably dressed seamen were serving drinks to the gathering with all the aplomb of expert restauranteurs.

"Wot'll you 'ave, sirs? Lemonade or rum punch?" A hirsute fellow handled a tea tray full of glasses in his great work-worn hands, more suited to hauling a rope in a heavy sea.

"Rum for me," said Holmes promptly, reaching for a glass with his slender hand. "And you, Watson?" I followed suit. "Jolly good," said Holmes. Thank you very much, bosun."

"Bosun's mate, actually, sir." But the man was pleased at the compliment.

Holmes sipped his drink. "Excellent," he observed. "Pusser rum, is it not?"

"Right, sir."

"Jamaica, one hundred and ten overproof."

"Right again, sir," the man grinned his approval.

Inevitably, I was surprised and impressed with Holmes' expertise in the matter. For years I had been aware of and shared my old friend's knowledge and taste in wine, brandy and sherry, but for him to suddenly emerge as a rum expert confounded me. Again, I was amused at his apparent present need to impress this simple fellow with his recondite knowledge. Yet certainly, in a moment, he had made friends, and had a willing ally.

Holmes sipped his drink again, and glanced about him. "Where is Sir Matthew, pray, bosun's mate?" he asked. "We must pay our respects."

"On the tennis courts, sir. At 'is age an' all!" With that the sailor moved away, dispersing the contents of his tray amidst the throng. Holmes and I strolled in the gardens, appreciating the gaiety and color of the atmosphere, the sunlight and warmth of the Pacific climate after the frigid prairie winter through which we had passed.

We followed the sound of tennis balls being struck, and rounding a clipped yew hedge we discovered a double tennis court upon which a game was being played. A tall, white-haired, robust figure of a man at this moment climaxed the competition by smashing the ball so swiftly and so accurately beyond his opponent's ability to reach it, that the ball hit the back line, and bounced vigourously in our direction.

Holmes snatched it out of mid-air. "Game and set, I believe," cried Holmes.

"And how d'you know that, sir? Appearing out of nowhere?" The tall white haired fellow seemed irascible.

Holmes advanced with a smile, ball in hand. "Merely the anguish on the face of your opponent, Sir Matthew," he said.

The young man against whom Begbie had been matched came forward, mopping his brow, reaching across the net to shake Sir Matthew's hand.

"Jolly good, sir. Thank you," he said. "Excuse me, gentlemen, I need a drink." He bowed in a courteous manner, and departed.

"Decent enough chaps, these naval officers. There's always some in port. They brighten the days for me in retirement, I must say!"

"In retirement, sir?" said Holmes. "That's not the word I had in Whitehall."

"Whitehall, eh?" Begbie scrutinized us suspiciously from under shaggy brows. "More confounded government officials?"

"Not exactly officials, Sir Matthew," said Holmes "And not exactly government."

"Then who the devil are the pair of you?"

"My friend and companion, Doctor Watson, and myself, Sherlock Holmes. Acting at the moment as emissaries to Her Majesty Queen Victoria, in her fair and far-flung Dominion of Canada."

"Good Lord!" Begbie looked at us, from one to the other. "What brings you all the way out here, then? Come, let us sit." He moved to some adjacent lawn chairs, placed beside a small round table, where at once an attentive steward served him with a tall drink, as if knowing his unspoken wish. "Thank you, George," said Begbie. He sat down, gesturing us to do the same thing. "Are you fellows drinking?"

Holmes and I held aloft our tumblers, still half full of the rum punch. We sat down.

"Ah. Next round perhaps," said Begbie, and he took an appreciative pull at his own glass.

"We are here, Sir Matthew, at the behest of Her Majesty Queen Victoria. Indeed, I have a personal communication for you from Her Gracious Majesty." Holmes reached inside his capacious inner pocket and produced an envelope, folded upon itself and sealed with regal looking, beribboned red wax.

Sir Matthew paused, his glass at his lips, his eyes on the missive in Holmes' hand. After a moment, he put the glass down on the table and reached out for the envelope. His fierce old eyes had become a little misty. "Excuse me, gentlemen," he said, his voice husky with emotion. "After these many years ... you see, I was quite ... close to Her

Sir Matthew Begbie

Majesty as a youth.... I thought, perhaps, I had fallen into disfavour with Her Majesty ..."

Holmes and I exchanged glances and excused ourselves, leaving the aging figure of Sir Matthew seated at his table, peering through his spectacles at the missive that Holmes had delivered to him.

I had heard something of this man's legendary past, his romantic, musical-poetic nature, his knowledge of languages, his unrequited love for an unidentified lady out of his reach, his singlehanded foray into the mountains and forests of British Columbia, to impose law and order in the Queen's name on one of the wildest communities of the time, in all likelihood saving this part of Her Majesty's far-flung Empire from absorption into the United States. And now to be passed over by the community he had help construct.

As Holmes and I rejoined the crowd of merry-makers, the Royal Navy band gave a formal flourish to the piece they were playing, and laid down their instruments. The audience in their fashionable dresses and smart uniforms turned and clapped their appreciation. The stewards moved through the throng with trays of refreshment. The air was full of eager anticipation.

What appeared to be a guard of honor had formed near the entrance to the garden, on either side of a red carpet. A senior officer displaying the gleaming broad gold stripe of rear-admiral wore his dress uniform, cocked hat and sword. Senior businessmen in top hats and morning coats crowded in.

A uniformed young man with the stripes of a lieutenant, Royal Navy, handsome of sun-tanned countenance and broad of shoulder, reached for a drink. The tray had just been presented to Holmes and myself, and our hands almost collided with that of the young officer.

"I beg pardon, gentlemen," he said, politely withdrawing his hand.

"Not at all," replied Holmes, placing his empty glass on the tray, and helping himself to a full one.

"I'm a bit nervous, you see," said the young man.

"I have observed that," replied Holmes.

The young officer took a fresh glass of the rum punch and emptied a third of it at a go.

"There seems to be a pleasurable excitement in the air," observed Holmes.

"The King of Siam is about to arrive. That's why I'm nervous."

"The King of Siam?" said Holmes.

"Chowa Chualalankorn."

"Chowa what?" I said.

"Chowa Chualalankorn," replied the lieutenant. "That's his name. I had the pleasure of attending him in Bangkok."

"Why are you nervous, may I ask?" said Holmes.

"Because I fell in love with one of his retinue, and she with me," said the young man. He finished his drink. "She's here today as one of the King's entourage. No end of a problem."

At this moment there was a brazen blast of trumpets, and the clash and thump of some Eastern instruments, sounding most exotic in this transplanted English atmosphere on the far coast of British Columbia.

The guard of naval ratings came smartly to rigid attention, the gates opened, and through them came an entourage of perhaps the most beautiful and elegant people I have had the privilege to observe. First came the members of a Siamese orchestra, carrying and playing their instruments, the musicians dressed in the most extravagantly colourful yet graceful costumes I have seen. Then a group of costumed maidens, the king's retinue, beautiful and elegant beyond my imagination. From their colouring, contours and facial appearance, they appeared to be from different Eastern racial origins. But all astonishingly beautiful, moving like the trained and talented dancers they undoubtedly were. I glanced at the young naval lieutenant, and followed his enraptured gaze towards a particularly beautiful creature, who, as part of the entourage, slender arms moving gently to the music, long golden fingernails, a curious pagoda-like structure on her elegant head, seemed absorbed in the rhythms of her sedate dance. Only her eyes betrayed her, long, black and shining, their dark beauty accentuated by the application of some agent, kohl perhaps. She met the young man's gaze with a subdued passion such as I have never seen before, and which brought an envious lump to my aging throat.

I glanced at Holmes. His eye was on a palanquin that was now entering the gate. A chair of some dark Eastern wood, with inlays of gold, silver and ivory, was being carried on poles, on the shoulders of half a dozen Siamese court followers, clothed in ceremonial robes. Seated on the chair was a man I took to be Chualalankorn himself, King of Siam. Small, quite young I should judge, bright of eye, dapper, he curiously enough was dressed in Western style, with top hat, a well-cut, hand tailored morning suit, a nicely tied foulard, and highly polished black shoes. It has always puzzled and disappointed me that the drab formal male garb of London and Paris is increasingly being adopted by Eastern ambassadors, who, to my mind, lose so much of their splendid uniqueness and originality by assuming Western dress in this manner.

With a clash of cymbals the entourage came to a halt. The bearers of the palanquin rested their burden upon the red carpet, and went down upon hands and knees, their faces to the ground in obeisance to their ruler, who now stepped from the conveyance with a sprightly gait. He was welcomed by the bemedalled Admiral, who, sword in hand, saluted the royal visitor most smartly.

One of the Siamese court attendants, a man of obvious authority, had remained standing, though bowing repeatedly in a most courtly fashion. He now, in his colorful native garb, and with sinuous movements of his slender hands, translated the greetings and salutations of the welcoming committee, and responses from the royal visitor.

"What is the purpose of Chualalankorn's visit to this outpost of Empire?" queried Holmes of the young lieutenant.

"He is a man of business," was the reply. "It is cheaper and faster, these days, to reach the Western markets of New York, London and Paris, by shipping goods across the Pacific, and by train across Canada — tea, spices, silk, and so on. He has accompanied the first shipment himself. Public relations, I've heard it called."

The young man's eye was on the maiden, who in company with her companions had sunk to the red carpet in a servile yet graceful fashion. "I really must work out some arrangement regarding the young lady," said our companion, with a worried expression on his visage. He gave us a smart salute, excused himself, and disappeared into the crowd.

The formalities of welcome being dispensed with, the King of Siam and his interpreter were escorted to a modest pavilion on the grounds where he was greeted by Sir Matthew, now formally attired in morning coat and silk hat. In company with the Western businessmen, they entered the building and were lost to view.

As if on a signal, the Siamese musicians now broke into a cacophony of sound, with a clashing of gongs, the clack of wooden hammers on an array of blocks of the same material, and the blast of wind

Chualalankorn himself, King of Siam ...

instruments, all unfamiliar to my Western ear. To these discordant strains, the beautiful maidens arose from their repose on the red carpet like flowers bursting into bloom, and with measured movements of grace and delight danced for the assembled Western company. The young lieutenant was nowhere to be seen.

CHAPTER TWO

Whale Hunt at Bella Coola

The following morning, in the pleasant Hotel Victoria where we were staying, Holmes and I had no sooner sat down to our bacon and eggs, toast and marmalade than a messenger entered, and without ceremony requested our early attendance upon Sir Matthew Begbie, who apparently urgently needed our assistance. A carriage was waiting for us. I barely had time for a second cup of excellent Travancore tea when Holmes, impatient as ever, hastened me along, and in a short time we were bowling through the fresh morning air.

Sir Matthew received us civilly enough. He was already out in his garden, ruefully surveying the damage to lawns and flower beds caused by yesterday's celebration. He was helping his gardener to clean up the inevitable debris of the event in which we had been privileged to participate.

"Holmes," said Sir Matthew, without preamble. "The King of Siam wants to go on a whale hunt."

"He what?" cried Holmes, somewhat surprised.

"To go on a whale hunt. He is a man of great curiosity, many skills and interests. He has heard that at this time of year, the whales frequent this part of the coast in great numbers."

"Yes?"

"And yesterday, business concluded, he pressed us with questions about the Indians of the West coast. The Bella Coola, of whom he had heard. He seems fascinated by stories of totem poles, war canoes and the like. Inadvertently I mentioned the whale hunt as performed by the Nootkas, in their great canoes, and in a most peremptory fashion he requested that I arrange one for him. He and his entourage are here for a day or two, in his ship, lying in the harbour."

"I see," said Holmes.

"The letter you brought me from the gracious Queen Victoria," Sir Matthew continued, "I might say, while being most welcome to me personally, also suggested that should the King of Siam arrive on my doorstep I should do everything within my power to meet his needs, whims and fancies, in the interest of international accord."

Holmes had filled his pipe with tobacco, and now lit it. He puffed out a cloud of smoke with apparent satisfaction. "I discussed the matter with Lieutenant Commander Cole-Hamilton, captain of the destroyer H.M.S. *Alert,* which is also lying in the harbour. He was part of the reception committee yesterday, for King Whatsisname."

"Chowa Chualalankorn," said Holmes.

"Yes," said Begbie. "Cole-Hamilton suggested that we could take the king up the coast to a Bella Coola village he is somewhat familiar with, and he can arrange with the chief the requested whale hunt. It might even cement relationships, one way or another. Our gracious Queen would approve, do you not think so?"

"I quite agree," said Holmes. "In what way could I be of assistance?"

"I was hoping you would offer your inestimable services, Holmes," was the response. "I am, of course, concerned with safety. Usually a foreign potentate passes through here quite formally, with little risk to life and limb."

I thought for a moment of the practice of allowing adventurous visitors to go through portions of the Rocky Mountains on the front bumper of the giant locomotives, over yawning mountain gorges and chasms and rushing cataracts; and of our recent adventure with Sarah Bernhardt.

A manservant in a white jacket appeared with a tray on which was a pot of coffee, cups, cream and sugar. He put it on a garden table. Begbie thanked him, and poured coffee for us.

"But in this case?" queried Holmes.

"In this case, Holmes?" Begbie's faded blue eyes peered quizzically from under ragged grey brows. "I know something of your reputation, you see." He sipped his coffee for a moment, then added some sugar. "In this case, I would be very happy if you were to accompany the party to Bella Coola, Holmes, and to attend to the safety of our charge, the King of Siam, until he is away from our care and responsibility."

And so it was that Holmes and I found ourselves sharing a small cabin in Her Majesty's Fleet Destroyer *Alert,* heading in a northerly direction, amidst the islands and the boisterous wind, sun and cloud, of the Briitish Columbia coast. We were invited to the bridge by the commanding officer, and while Holmes was being introduced to some of the elements of navigation, I found myself in conversation with the young lieutenant with whom Holmes and I had previously conversed at the reception.

He introduced himself as Broughton-Smythe of Kent, following in the sea-going tradition of his family, dating back to Nelson's time.

"How goes your passionate love affair?" I asked him, outspokenly enough. After all, it was he who had confided in Holmes and myself in the first place.

"Fa-ying?" he said. He glanced at me with a sudden smile, the sun dancing on the sea behind him. Across the channel, the dark primeval forest, shrouded in mist, came down to the waterline. The young officer checked the compass course of the vessel, and glanced at a navigation chart. "I am concerned for her," he said, confident that the ship was on the correct course. "Before going on this expedition, Chualalankorn sent all his staff back to his ship, other than the two or three he has on board here. Fa-ying was one of them. I don't know how to extricate her." Our attention was diverted by a sudden turbulence some distance off our port bow.

"I say," he cried. "Whales!" We watched the creatures as they surfaced and blew great sparkling fountains of water into the sunlight. "Care to look?" He handed me his binoculars.

I watched with considerable fascination, as the great creatures surfaced, blew, and submerged again. "If you were able to, as you say, 'extricate' your young lady, what would be your future together?" I ventured: Across my mind flashed a recollection of more than one brief, passionate relationship of my own youth, disrupted by inflexible elements of time and geography.

"I could put in for service in Siam. I believe there are opportunities for advancement, serving our good Queen in those parts."

... a community unlike any I had seen ...

The destroyer had cleared a series of islands, and now, at reduced speed, she swung into a new vista, which opened before us disclosing a community unlike anything I had seen before. Set against the primeval forest on the edge of the sea were low extensive wooden buildings, the supporting members of which appeared to be great tree trunks carved and painted in the most imaginative and wondrous fashion. I had heard of the totem figures of the Indians of Western Canada, as remarkable works of art. But to be confronted with them, not as museum pieces, but as significant elements in a living community, touched me deeply.

I had retained the binoculars, and through their magnifying lenses the totems leaped into focus. Against the great mountains, blue with distance, carved poles by the score stood out in the vagrant sunshine, with their emblems of raven and whale, and many grotesque figures I could not identify. As I watched, I saw great war canoes fully fifty feet in length launched into the sea, each manned by two score dark-skinned warriors, who with great dexterity and speed, maneuvered their slender craft towards us.

Our captain, seemingly satisfied with the position of his vessel, now stopped engines, and going slowly astern, signaled the fo'c'sle party to drop anchor. With a splash and the rumble of chain, the hook went over the side, and presently we were brought up, swinging gently to the tide.

On the quarterdeck of the ship, the first lieutenant now stood in company with the King of Siam and his attendants, who had been quartered in the captain's day cabin until now. The potentate's top hat and dress coat had been replaced with native Siamese garb – a "panang," so I have been told, a single piece of cloth of dark and intricate design, about a yard wide, and three yards in length, wrapped around his youthful body in a most sophisticated manner.

His Royal Highness was equipped with a chair of great craftsmanship and ornamentation, which his attendants supplied for his comfort, a throne of such a height, that sitting on it, his august head was higher than those attending him. Here he sat, as the war canoes came foaming towards us, the lithe brown bodies of the paddlers gleaming in the sun. In the bows of the canoe stood awe-inspiring figures, one wearing feathers and the carved visage of a voracious looking raven, the other representing some awesome symbolic creature of the woods, which I did not recognize. Suffice it to say that I felt transported by the display.

The canoes themselves, each of which I understood to be carved out of a single giant cedar tree, were creations of wonder. With their high curved prow and tapered stem, they were excellent sea-boats. Each was painted with colourful designs, representing mythical figures reflecting the highly sophisticated nature of these people.

It would seem that word had already been passed that we wished to participate in a whale hunt, for the canoes were already prepared, and equipped with harpoons – lances, fully twenty feet in length, that lay pointing over the bows of the slender vessels, ready for action. As I was to discover on closer acquaintance, the heads of the lances were fitted with large pieces of shaped and sharpened mussel shell, cut in notches and spliced to the slender poles. Upon impact with the whale, these sharp blades would detach themselves from the shaft of the harpoon, and, being buoyed up by inflated bladders of sealskin, prevent the unfortunate creature from diving. Thus the canoes could move in, and administer the *coup de grâce*.

I must add that I was able to observe that the hunters themselves were remarkably formal in their relationship to their prey, as with prayers and ceremonies appropriate to the occasion they begged the creatures' pardon, recognizing that man, animal, forest, fish and ocean, are all one and inter-dependent under the Great Spirit.

Presently the canoes were alongside, and the Nootka chief — the one with the raven head-dress — had swarmed up the jumping ladder in a most agile fashion. He was received on the quarterdeck by our doughty captain, piped aboard by the bosun's mate, and saluted smartly by the ship's officers, drawn up to attend his arrival. He came to rest, his bare feet planted on the ship's immaculate deck, his raven plumes blowing in the wind. The chief was a man approaching middle age, tall, slender, and well-muscled, quite six feet in height. Through the mask, his dark eyes gleamed with eager anticipation. His bare palms came up in a gesture of salutation. The captain stepped forward, right hand outstretched, and the chief took it in his own.

"Welcome, Captain," he said in excellent English, "I received your message. It has come at a convenient time. The whales are gathering." His bright eyes turned to King Chualalankorn, seated upon his portable throne, surrounded by his minions.

"Chief Ondonaga," replied the Captain, "may I introduce you to our guest, Chowa Chualalankorn, King of Siam." He turned to the seated royal figure. "Your Excellency," he said, "may I present Chief Ondonaga of the Nootka tribe, here on the coast of British Columbia. The chief is very pleased to welcome you as a guest, and as a participant in the whale hunt, as you requested."

It was an extraordinary moment, this meeting of two absolute rulers from two such different cultures, half a world apart. The king's interpreter started to translate the captain's words, but to my surprise, Chualalankorn held up one bejewelled hand, and the man stopped in mid-sentence, and bowed apologetically to the floor boards. The tiny Oriental King then rose from his chair, and stepped down onto the deck, where he was dwarfed in size by the Indian chief.

"I am most pleased to be here, Chief Ondonaga," he said in halting but excellent English, "as your guest, and the guest of the Royal Navy." He bowed to the Captain, who returned his salute by bringing his heels together smartly, and inclining his head. "I am quite ready for the adventure. Am I dressed ... what is the word?" He looked around for his advisor.

"Appropriately, sir," said the latter, happy to be of service.

"Yes?" said Chualalankorn.

"Most appropriately, sir," replied the chief with delicacy. "Although perhaps the Captain would be good enough to provide oil-skins, in case it is a little damp in the canoe."

And, oilskins readily provided, we were privileged to embark upon this adventure, hunting the great whale of the Pacific, in Indian dugout canoes fifty feet in length, seven or eight feet in beam, with a crew of fifty warriors in each.

CHAPTER THREE

The Noble Lieutenant

In my time, I have seen something of the sea, as ship's doctor on the *Orontes* to India, and in the old *Fastnet* around Cape Horn, but never before had I experienced the sensation of sitting in a giant native dugout canoe, my bottom at the very waterline, being propelled over the face of the sea by the muscular exertions of two dozen painted Indian warriors on each side of the boat.

The school of whales that we had spotted from the bridge of H.M.S. *Alert* were seemingly not unusual at this time of year, on this particular coast. Breeding in the far north, the giant mammals come down from the Bering Sea, through the straits and channels between the offshore islands and the mainland, and in doing so for untold centuries of time, have supplied the West Coast Indians with a staple part of their diet. It is almost as if, over time, there had developed an understanding between them — the hunter and the hunted — for the passage of the whale is quite predictable, and when the great canoes surge out to attack, there appears to be little effort made by the great beasts to taking avoiding action.

And so it was this day. The canoes took us off the destroyer, Chualalankorn and Holmes with the Chief in the bows of one of them, myself and Lieutenant Broughton-Smythe with the chief's son in the

Nootka Tribe

other. We set off at a brave pace in a northerly direction up the coast, where the blue headlands appeared to converge. Under the paddlers' powerful thrusts, we surged rapidly ahead, meeting the long Pacific rollers in bursting showers of sparkling spray.

Seated as I was with Broughton-Smythe in the bows of the vessel, I indeed had a ringside seat. Only the chief's son, a lad barely out of his teens, was in front of us in the high curving bow, readying his lances, spear-heads, raw-hide ropes and sealskin floats, ready for the coming action.

I glanced over at the other canoe. It was perhaps twenty feet away, slightly ahead of us, its slender bows lifting with every measured stroke of the warriors, moving together, grunting in unison. High in the bows I could see Chief Ondonaga's dark form silhouetted against the sunlit sea. He was peering ahead towards the gap opening up between the two headlands. On the thwart immediately behind him sat Chualalankorn and Holmes. I was initially surprised that the former had dismissed his followers for the adventure, retaining only the services of my friend Sherlock Holmes, but I think the King was a most practical man, and since he desired to participate in a whale hunt, he recognized that this was the best way to do so.

I suspect also, that when Chualalankorn had first voiced his wish to Sir Matthew Begbie, the latter, in his eagerness to fulfill his duty to the Queen, had seized upon the known qualities of Holmes, as opposed to the unknown virtues of members of the King's staff, and had convinced Chualalankorn of Holmes' superior dependability.

In any event, bounding over the shining sea on this early summer day, the two canoes converged on an opening between two islands, and there, lifting out of the deep, were the dark forms of the creatures we had come to pursue. A pod of perhaps five or six sperm whales, twenty feet or more in length, lifted lazily on the ocean swell, blowing clouds of spray into the air, slapping the ocean's surface with their great tails, submerging, then repeating the process, as if in social intercourse.

Not a word was spoken in the two canoes. The paddlers at once increased their exertions, and the great craft leaped ahead at each stroke. In the bows of the canoes, the chief in one, his young son in the other, quietly prepared to strike.

One of the bigger whales had surfaced, a little apart from its companions, and at a gesture from the chief the canoes adjusted their course towards it. Seemingly unaware of our presence, or perhaps knowingly accepting its role in this ancient ritual, the creature first submerged, then, as we closed the spot where it had disappeared, suddenly emerged from the sea in a burst of spray and broken water, its great head rearing above us for a moment before plunging again into the deep, its long smooth back glistening in the sunlight.

But in that fraction of time, the paddlers had stopped the momentum of their noble craft, and in the bows of each the chief and his son moved powerfully and with precision, planting their lances deep into the flesh of the magnificent beast.

The long razor-like blades of mussel shell found their mark, and, detaching themselves from the lances, pulled the inflated bladders of sealskin overboard, to inhibit the diving of our prey once more into the deep. The sea was at once tossed into a welter of bloodstained foam, as the great beast lifted the dark flukes of its tail, and smashed the surface of the turbulent waters. Again the harpoons struck, and blood stained the sea. The sealskin bladders went over the side. The great creature was pouring blood, attempting to dive, but its equilibrium was destroyed by the counter-buoyancy of the inflated sealskins.

From both canoes, a third harpoon attack rained upon the whale, then, as the accompanying sealskins flew overboard, I was aware of a sudden frantic commotion in the other canoe. My scalp crawled as I realized what had occurred. In the crowded confines of the vessel, and the excitement of the moment, the raw-hide line which attached the sealskin bladder to the lethal harpoon blade had become entangled in the legs of Chualalankorn, and that gentleman had been pulled over the side of the boat, and was now on the glistening back of the whale. Unable to release himself, he was hanging grimly onto one of the harpoons embedded in the creature's flesh.

In a moment, I saw Holmes rise from his place in the canoe, revolver in hand, and leap onto the body of the monster, just behind its head. Grasping yet another of the imbedded harpoons to avoid being swept into the sea, he emptied the contents of his pistol into the beast's eye. A great shudder convulsed the creature, and Holmes turned his attention to Chualalankorn. His Majesty, I must say, seemed cool enough, but his leg was firmly entrapped by the tough raw-hide thong attached to the buoyant sealskins. Holmes pulled desperately at the thong in vain, and looked around in distress.

Then I felt a movement beside me. It was Lieutenant Broughton-Smythe, who, dirk in hand, leaped without hesitation upon the whale's back, and, literally running the length of the creature, reached Holmes and the entrapped royal figure. I saw the young officer crouch down, and with a single powerful stroke, sever the restraining raw-hide line.

In a moment Holmes and the lieutenant between them had helped the King of Siam back into the relative safety of the canoe in which I sat.

Chief Ondonaga, in the other canoe, speaking in his own tongue, gave swift instructions to his son, who responded at once by casting off from the whale, and taking us back in rapid order to the destroyer, which was still lying at anchor.

CHAPTER FOUR

The Matter Is Resolved

The young King Chualalankorn seemed buoyed up by his experience. In dry clothes, in the wardroom, drinking hot rum with melted butter and cinnamon, he got quite merry, enacting for the ship's officers and his own staff the happenings of the day, with gesture and graphic verbal description in both English and Siamese. Holmes and Lieutenant Broughton-Smyth, both now in dry clothing, tumblers of hot rum steaming in their hands, exchanged glances of amusement, and I'm sure of relief, at the happy conclusion to what could have been an international incident of considerable proportions.

Presently, his dramatic performance concluded to the clapping of his faithful staff and the wardroom officers, Chualalankorn placed his empty rum glass on the silver tray of the wardroom steward. "And now," said his Highness in his careful English, "I must express my deep gratitude and appreciation to you, Mr. Holmes, for your extraordinary service to me today. As a small token of my gratitude, please accept this ring. It belonged to my grandfather, the great Chowfa Mongkat."

At the mention of the name, the Siamese staff members, with an exhalation of breath, bowed deeply to the floor, hands clasped before them.

"I now present it to you, Mr. Holmes," concluded his Majesty, and so saying he took a ring from his royal finger and placed it in my friend's outstretched palm.

"I am most honored, Your Highness," said Holmes. "I shall wear it with pride." With a flourish, Holmes placed the ring on his own finger, and bowed deeply to our royal companion.

There was a round of applause at this, and the King of Siam turned to young Lieutenant Broughton-Smythe. "And you, young man," said the monarch. "Had it not been for your brave, swift action, all might have been lost. In what way do I demonstrate my deep thanks to you?"

Broughton-Smythe blushed deeply, came to attention, and made no reply. The King glanced at the Captain for guidance, and the Captain said, "Lieutenant, you must have some desire."

"I have, sir," said the young man. "A deep desire."

"What is it then?" said the Captain. "Speak up."

"It is the hand of the Princess Fa-ying, of the Royal Court of Siam, in marriage," responded the youth.

The diminutive Chualalankorn looked somewhat askance at this, and in his native tongue, he spoke to his vizier for some moments. The latter bowed, and responded in soothing accents.

"His Highness states that he recognizes how truly attractive is the Princess Fa-ying, and he understands how the young lieutenant should fall under her spell. But His Highness is a most practical man, and he asks where would the happy couple dwell, the lieutenant upon the tumultuous seas, and the bride far away in one land or another? Surely that would not be satisfactory for anyone."

The Captain looked at Broughton-Smythe for an answer; receiving no response, he turned to Sherlock Holmes. "Holmes?" he queried.

"Are there not Royal Navy appointments to the court of Siam these days?" replied my friend.

"I am not aware of such," replied the Captain.

"Surely such a role would be of considerable value to Her Majesty's Empire, in these parlous times, helping to cement East-West relations."

"My word, Holmes, I think you have it! East-West relations in these parlous times! I shall make such a recommendation to the Lords of the Admiralty." He turned to the young lieutenant who stood before him at rigid attention. "Would that be satisfactory to you, Broughton-Smythe?"

"Aye, aye, sir!" said the young man in ringing tones. "Most satisfactory, sir!"

Chualalankorn had been following the conversation with concern. He now smiled most broadly, and bowed with clasped hands, first to the Captain, then to Holmes and Broughton-Smythe. "Then it is settled," he said. "Thank you gentlemen."

He clapped his hands, and his entourage faithfully followed suit, smiling, bowing and clapping their hands.

Back in Victoria, Sir Matthew Begbie was highly entertained by our report, and much relieved at the fortunate outcome.

"I shall report it to Her Majesty," he said. "Her Majesty will surely be pleased." Then he wanted to know what was next on Holmes' agenda.

"Has there not been another gold strike in this remarkable country?" asked Holmes. He was lighting his pipe, and the smoke curled round his aquiline features and half-closed eyes.

"In the Kootenays," replied Begbie. "Quite like old times, by all reports. Hurdy-gurdy girls, music, and dancing all night. Gold dust and nuggets. I haven't seen that sort of thing for many a year. The thought of it makes the old blood stir in the veins."

"How does one get up there, may I ask?"

"Stagecoach through the Fraser Canyon. Quite safe to travel these days," the old man's eyes lit up under their shaggy brows. "You're not thinking of going, are you Holmes?"

Holmes blew a cloud of smoke into the air. "It would be a pity to come all this way from England and not participate in such an event," he said. "What d'you say, Watson? Are you game?"

"I say 'jolly good'," I replied promptly.

Sir Matthew looked at us with a glint in his eye. "I say," he said. "Do you chaps mind if I come along?"

5

The Case of the Smiling Buddha

CHAPTER ONE

The Man in the Stagecoach

Our stagecoach careered along the Cariboo Road in imminent peril, it seemed to me, of plunging over the edges of the precipice into the turbulent rapids of the Fraser River far below.

Holmes' pipe had gone out, and he busied himself with his penknife removing the dottle. Then, half-opening the carriage window, he tossed out the charred remnants of burned tobacco, which blew away over the sheer rock cliff along which we travelled. Into the fug of our lurching conveyance came a blast of cold, damp air, and a fine rain which blurred the rugged mountain landscape through which we passed.

I was aware of our fellow-traveller leaning forward from the seat opposite, a heavy taciturn man in his mid-fifties, his face seared with an unremitting life in the outdoors, large hands blunted and calloused by manual labour. On his left hand he wore a heavy ring, set with a gold nugget. As he moved, the light caught the back of his hand and the gleaming ring, its shape resembling a human skull.

As I watched, the man reached out his hand, thumb extended, and deliberately squashed a mosquito on the partly lowered window. "Gol durn bloodsucker," he enunciated. He withdrew his hand, leaving a splotch of blood on the windowpane.

Sherlock Holmes glanced at the action, seemingly interested in the blood stain on the mud-splashed window.

Our fellow-traveller, from under grizzled brows peered out into the mist. He spoke in a hoarse voice, as if to himself. "Back in '63," he said, "I come down this here trail with over thirty thousand pounds sterling worth of gold." The carriage lurched in its passage, and I braced myself to keep my balance.

"My word," I said.

Holmes closed the window and was re-charging his pipe. "Yours?" he queried.

"What?" said our fellow-passenger.

"The gold," replied Holmes.

"Oh," said the man. "The gold." It was as if he had dismissed what he had said a moment ago as an aberration, and our conveyance went on for some distance before he spoke again. "No," he said. "The gold wasn't mine." He sat back in his corner, and wrapped himself in a sea-farer's cape that had seen better days. A moment or two passed, then he spoke again in a somewhat anguished voice. "Officially," he said, "the gold belonged to a fellow called Percy Van Sickle. In three months up there in the Barker Creek area, he got six hundred and fifty pounds weight from the Red Crow claim. It was all his, every ounce of it." He emitted a sound that was between a laugh and a groan of anguish. "That was the story, anyways. I was there at the time, diggin' my heart out, believin' I was a partner." He paused again, while our coach rattled on. Then, in a more controlled voice, he continued, "We took the gold down the trail here, to Vancouver, in a bullock wagon, with an escort of about twenty men on foot. Clear down this road here. I was one of the escort."

Holmes blew out a plume of smoke. "Any trouble?" he said.

"Trouble?" replied our companion.

"A lonely road through rugged wilderness. A fortune in gold. A wild and lawless land."

"Oh, I see what you mean. No, no trouble. It was back in the days of the Hanging Judge." Our companion said this as if it explained everything.

"The Hanging Judge?" said Holmes.

"Begbie," was the response.

I glanced at the fourth occupant of our carriage. Sir Matthew Begbie snored gently in a corner seat, his cape around his aging shoulders.

"Now there was a man!" exclaimed our fellow-traveller. "Appointed by Queen Victoria herself, to bring law and order into these parts." The careering carriage lurched over a particularly uneven patch of roadway. There were leather straps hanging conveniently inside our conveyance, to which one could cling, and thus avoid being flung about by the erratic motion. I grasped one of them.

"Before Begbie arrived, there were fellows in the gold fields who would cut your throat for your poke. Rascals from the Barbary Coast, Chinese coolies brought in to build the railway, fortune hunters from Eastern Canada and England. There was opium and booze aplenty. Things got so bad the Americans threatened to take over to protect their own citizens. Then Begbie come in on his big black stallion, and straightened out the hull shebang single-handed, and saved British Columbia fer the Queen, God bless 'er!"

"Really!"

I was impressed with the heart-felt utterance of our fellow-traveller. I glanced at Sir Matthew, and observed that he had stopped snoring.

"It must be twenty years ago in Barker Creek, I seen Begbie tellin' a jury that had just acquitted a man, that they all deserved to hang!" Our companion gave a hoarse laugh at the memory. "I just wish I could've got to 'im on the claim I was done out of! But those days have gone."

Sir Matthew's eyes had opened and were glinting with sharp interest. "And what is your name, sir?" The question was directed at our fellow-traveller.

The man looked at Begbie, surprised and a little defensive. "Sam O'Shaunessy is the name."

"Ah yes." Sir Matthew stroked his beard for a moment, his eyes searching the other's face. "Sea captain in command of the Black Ball line *Sarah McDonald* when that ship took fire at sea. Came ashore and staked an area adjacent to the Van Sickle, claim. Sank a shaft to fifty-four feet and ran a seventy-eight foot drift. Dug and hauled every bucketful by hand. Coarse gold. Van Sickle claimed possession."

O'Shaunessy's face was a sight to see. His jaw fell, his mouth gaped, his pale blue eyes widened in amazement and filled with unbidden tears. His work-worn hands came up and covered his face.

Holmes, his own eyes hooded, sat back in his corner of the careering coach, wreathed in pipe smoke, observing the scene.

CHAPTER TWO

Sourdough Alley

The rain had ceased, and our coach and four, mud spattered and begrimed with its journey from Vancouver, swung into Sourdough Alley, the main street of Rossland. A lurid placard hung outside a self-proclaimed theatre, portraying two muscular individuals braced for a prizefight. Next door was a gaming house, promising keno. Pack horses loaded with trail-worn gear and supplies threaded their way past a queue of men who stood patiently in front of a ramshackle building marked "Surveyor's Office." Another building displayed placards in English and in Chinese, offering the services of the Chinese Freemason Lodge. Two signs in Chinese hung vertically, one on either side of the door. Holmes looked at them with interest.

"'Looking in front is my mountain range with its green tops'," he said. "Most poetic."

"Really, Holmes," I said, impressed in spite of myself.

"And the other one says, 'Inside Buddha sits dignified.'"

My friend constantly surprises me with obscure fragments of knowledge, and I was about to question him further, but our coach had pulled up in front of the hotel, through whose open doors came the sound of merriment.

"Our accommodation," said Sir Matthew. "Though the best Rossland has to offer is somewhat primitive perhaps for you gentlemen so recently from the gracious city of London."

"My word!" replied Holmes. "I assure you, Sir Matthew, that this is a great adventure for us both, do you not agree, Watson? We are privileged to be here."

I could not but approve. Indeed, I had not seen my dear friend Sherlock Holmes looking so bright and relaxed for some time. It was as if he had shrugged off his habitual craving for the excitement of the chase, and felt the better for it.

Our fellow-traveller, Sam O'Shaunessy, had grasped his kit-bag, opened the coach door, and was about to get down.

"Mr. O'Shaunessy," said Begbie.

The man paused and turned, a look of anguish on his lined face. "Sir Matthew?" he said, civilly enough.

"If you wish, I shall endeavour to look into the rights and wrongs of your affair as you explained it to me, and report the findings to you."

"After all this time, sorr?" There was a hopeless tone in his voice.

"Better now than never."

"I thought to settle it meself, sorr, one way or t'other."

Looking at the man's powerful shoulders moving under his seaman's cape, and at the heavy work-callused hands with which he grasped his baggage and a cudgel-like walking stick, I thought that I would not care for him as an adversary, should it come to it.

"As you wish," said Begbie. "Good luck to you!"

The man gave a seaman's salute, the golden skull gleaming on his finger. He turned and was lost in the crowd.

The arrival of our coach had created a stir on the narrow streets of Rossland. In a moment crowds had gathered, pressing around the lathered horses and peering into the vehicle to see who the new arrivals might be. A hotel employee was worried about a shipment of champagne that appeared to be missing. Half a dozen Celestials in pigtails were smiling and bowing a welcome to a fellow Chinese who had been riding on top of the coach with the driver. Canvas mail bags were hauled out and signed for. Holmes, Sir Matthew and I climbed gratefully out of the stuffy confines of the carriage and claimed our baggage, which was handed down from the roof.

Bag in hand, I now turned to Holmes, and found him stooped over, magnifying glass to his eye, studying the bloody imprint of our recent travelling companion's thumb, which had dried on the window of the carriage we had just vacated.

"I say, Holmes. What are you up to?"

"Here, Watson, Sir Matthew," said Sherlock Holmes, "is an excellent exhibit of the way the epidermis of the human hand is traversed in various directions by depressions and friction ridges, arches, loops, whorls and so forth. Each pattern quite distinctive."

Sir Matthew peered through the lens.

"A simple thumbprint providing absolute identification of its owner. Different from every other thumbprint in the world," he went on.

"The Bertillon System," I said.

The Cariboo Road

"Quite." Holmes put away his glass and picked up his bag. "With an efficient photographic method to record and classify human finger-prints for cross reference, one could perhaps help to stem the growing world wide tide of criminal activity." Through the hubbub of the crowd, the movement of horses and mules in the road, the coming and going of pedestrians on the board sidewalk, I could now hear from inside the hotel strains of a dance band playing some popular air, accompanied by the thump of feet, female laughter and sporadic cries of approval. In company with Sir Matthew, Holmes and I made our way into the lobby.

It was spacious enough, a few chairs flanked by the ever-present "spittoons" I have observed in this country. Behind a counter a young fellow in his shirt-sleeves, brilliantined hair and a full mustache, presided over a registry-book, a pen, a pot of ink, a bell which sounded when one struck the metal plunger, and a board full of room keys. He had a perky air of authority, and looked up as we approached.

When Sir Matthew identified himself, this person was at once virtually contorted with bows and facial grimaces, meant, I am sure, to be ingratiating.

Yes, Sir Matthew and gentlemen, the best rooms in the house would be made available. He would send up a chambermaid to change the sheets and air the rooms. He would look after our baggage personally. In the meantime, while things were being prepared for our accommodation, perhaps we would like to relax in the bar. Giving voice to all this, he struck the bell several times with considerable vigour, giving instructions to a pair of chambermaids, and thrusting the registry book, pen and ink before us as if for the signing of a document of state.

Sir Matthew, bright of eye, lit a cigar and gave us a wink. "Just like old times," he said.

The term "wild west" had been recently coined, and although in my passage across Canada I had encountered various sorts of wildness, there was an abandon in the Rossland Hotel I had never before experienced, fuelled, no doubt, by the overwhelming lure and glittering presence of gold. Many of the men in the place in which we now found ourselves, instead of money of the realm, carried a small rawhide bag — a "poke" — containing gold dust, with which they made their purchases. The fellows behind the bar appeared to be most adroit at weighing out the amount of dust required to buy a round of drinks, a bottle of champagne, a meal of steak and potatoes, or a contribution for the ladies in the band.

Wending our way through the crowded tables and their boisterous occupants, Begbie, Holmes and I found ourselves a vacant table a little to one side, and ordered beer to wash away the dust of the Cariboo Road. A moment later a door under the gallery had opened, and a man somewhat younger than Sir Matthew emerged.

"Begbie!" he cried, crossing over to us. "I saw you come in! My word! How long is it? What brings you here?"

The men embraced each other heartily, Begbie towering over the other's diminutive form.

"May I introduce Sherlock Holmes and Doctor Watson," said Begbie. "Gentlemen, meet an old acquaintance of mine, Hardrock McKinnon."

"Welcome to you both, I'm sure," said McKinnon.

"These gentlemen are from London," went on Begbie. "They come to the Cariboo, curious about the way of life on the Canadian frontier."

"You come at an opportune moment, gentlemen," was the response. "A new vein of gold has just been opened up on the old Van Sickle property. Quite an exciting development." He rubbed his hands together. I noticed how big they were in proportion to his lithe figure. "I worked that property myself many years ago," he said.

He waved down a passing waiter and ordered whisky and cigars. "I made enough to open a small hotel, and I haven't handled a shovel since!"

He looked about with satisfaction. The band had just finished a ragtime tune, and the predominantly male audience seated around tables laden with wine and beer, caribou steaks and boiled potatoes, applauded vigorously. The plump chorus girls, all smiles and perspiration, mingled with their admirers.

"The Van Sickle property," said Holmes thoughtfully. "Did you not mention that name earlier, Sir Matthew?"

"Yes, I did," said Begbie shortly.

McKinnon glanced from Holmes to Begbie, a question on his lips. His attention was diverted by the waiter returning with his order and placing it upon the table.

"Fine Cuban," said our host, opening the box of cigars, and offering its contents. "Do have one."

"Sam O'Shaunessy worked the property years ago after it had been abandoned," said Begbie. "Then Van Sickle reclaimed it. Some technicality of registry. These things happen." He rolled a cigar between thumb and forefinger. He sniffed it. "Nice cigar."

"Only the best," said our host. A match flared in his fingers. He looked thoughtful. The band had started up again, playing a sentimental waltz.

Holmes puffed appreciatively. "So today the so-called Van Sickle property is worth millions, I take it," he said, eyes hooded.

"That's right," said our host, lighting up.

"And this fellow, O'Shaunessy, has no claim upon it?" Holmes pressed his point.

"None at all."

"He was in the stagecoach today," said Holmes.

"Was he?" Hardrock looked up sharply.

"Yes. He came into town with us. He said he had a claim to settle."

Our host frowned at this information, but there the matter remained. As guests of the establishment, we were wined and dined that evening most generously. After caribou steaks and quite a good red wine, we were joined by two or three of the ladies, and by a few old-time prospectors who had known Begbie in his earlier days. Our host, Hardrock McKinnon, excused himself presently, pleading business. Sir Matthew, despite his advancing years, proved to have a fine baritone voice, and to the accompaniment of the orchestra sang a number of ballads, much to the enjoyment of those present.

It was not until later in the evening that we gained our rooms, to discover that despite the lack of some civilized amenities we were quite comfortably off. Holmes and I were lodged in a double room, two beds, two chairs, a wash-basin and chamber-pot. Sir Matthew was in another just down the hall.

We had barely claimed our accommodation, however, when there came a tap on the door. I rose to open it. In the narrow hall there stood one of the dancers from the dining room, a young lady of comely aspect, a black lace shawl thrown over her bare shoulders, partly concealing her abbreviated costume.

"Mr. Holmes?" she queried.

"Holmes?" I said.

"Yes. The famous detective."

This was a surprise. Although Sir Matthew had introduced us to the hotel proprietor by name, there had been no mention of Holmes' profession. Indeed, since he was officially deceased, we had deliberately kept his identity quiet.

"I — er — " Thus challenged, I was not sure what to answer.

"Show her in, Watson." Holmes' crisp voice cut through my indecision.

The young lady met my eye with quiet self-assurance. I stood aside and she swept past me with the poise of a ballet dancer.

"I saw the Vancouver paper the coach brought," she said to Holmes, coming at once to the point. "It mentions you." She gave Holmes a column clipped from the newspaper.

He took it and swiftly read its contents. "Good Lord, Watson. Look at this!" he barked. He thrust the piece of newsprint at me and stalked about the room, feeling in his pocket for pipe and tobacco.

"Famous detective comes back," read the column. *"It has been revealed that the renowned English sleuth Sherlock Holmes, reported to have been drowned last year in the Reichenbach Falls, popular tourist resort in Switzerland, is in fact alive and well, and is at present visiting British Columbia as the guest of Sir Matthew Begbie, Queen Victoria's representative in these parts. Holmes is accompanied by Doctor Watson, who, as followers of Sherlockian adventures are aware, is the chronicler of the same gentleman."*

"Not very well written, is it?" I commented.

"'Chronicler of the same gentleman?'"

"Really, Watson. You aren't much help —" snarled Holmes. He snatched the document from my hand. "I must get in touch with the Foreign Office. For the first time I fail to read a newspaper, and I see this!"

Our young visitor stood quietly watching the performance. "If you are the courteous Sherlock Holmes that Doctor Watson has written about," she said, "perhaps you might be good enough to ask me to sit down."

Holmes turned to her, curbing his impatience. The two chairs with which our sparse room was equipped, were already occupied with his belongings, coat on one, travelling bag on the other. He flung the coat onto his bed, and deposited his bag on the floor.

"Please, ma'am," he said. "Do sit down."

"Thank you, sir," said the young lady, and gracefully she did so, arranging the long black shawl so as to conceal, at least in part, her shapely limbs.

Holmes proceeded to stuff his pipe with tobacco, his eyes now on our visitor, I think with some appreciation of her grace and beauty, but also, if I am any judge, with a certain sense of challenge. The females who over the years have come to my friend for assistance have usually been modest ladies, used in the main to a formal position in society, and certainly fully dressed. The young creature now before us, although most correct in her conduct and her manner of speech, had a directness and an independence of expression which was unusual, and as I have already observed, even with the Spanish shawl around her, revealed a most startling and attractive figure.

Holmes got his pipe going, and sat in the other chair. "May I ask your name?"

Barkerville B.C., 1860

"I am Dolores O'Shaunessy," replied the lady. "I believe you travelled from Vancouver with my father."

"Ah, yes," said Holmes. "Samuel O'Shaunessy. He is well, I trust." He regarded the lady through a cloud of tobacco smoke, his grey eyes glinting with sudden interest.

"I have only seen him briefly since his return, but I am concerned for him. He seemed to me like a man at the end of his tether. He was on his way to the Van Sickle mine, I was led to understand. He gave me an envelope. I thought you might like to see its contents."

Holmes held out his hand, and from under her shawl, with an elegant and unselfconscious movement of her slender arm, the lady produced what appeared to be a letter. Holmes took it from her and held it in his hand for a moment.

My friend has moments of concentration which still fascinate me after all these years. He did not at once open the envelope. Instead he raised it to his nose and sniffed it, front and back, and indeed along the edges. Then, rising abruptly, he went to the gas lamp sticking out of the wall, and held the envelope against the light. He scrutinized it through his magnifying glass.

"Excellent hand-made rice paper of Chinese manufacture. Quite old. From Yuan province, I should say."

"That is very likely, Mr. Holmes," the lady responded. "My father was, as they say in the trade, a 'China Coast skipper.' Years ago."

"May I ask what you were expected to do with this?"

"I was to take it to Mr. Wong at the Chinese Freemason Lodge."

"You mentioned its contents."

"Yes. A note from my father to me in English, and a document in what appears to be Chinese, presumably for Mr. Wong's interest."

"May I see the papers?"

"Indeed, Mr. Holmes, I brought them to you for that purpose."

Holmes opened the envelope, and extracted two folded sheets of paper. He held them up and scrutinized them. "One," he said. "A sheet of paper torn from a common writing tablet one can buy in any stationery shop. The other an excellent make of rice paper, of some age, contemporary with the envelope which contains it." Holmes unfolded the more modest of the documents. "This is a most personal note, Miss O'Shaunessy," he said after a moment of perusal. "Addressed to yourself. Are you sure that I should read it?"

"I would be privileged if you would," replied the lady. "Aloud, if you please, so that Doctor Watson may learn of its contents, and understand my concern."

Holmes turned again to the document. *"My darling Dolores,"* he read aloud. *"It is a cruel irony that they have now struck gold worth millions of dollars in the old Van Sickle mine, where I laboured so hard and so long for a pittance. As you know, I was one of the original partners with Van Sickle in the mine. But such are the vagaries of chance and the law in these parts, that there seems now to be no official record of our original agreement, and I am left out in the cold, as they say.*

"I gather that Van Sickle is presently in these parts, although aging, like myself, and I am seeking him out to reason with him. It is not for me, at my time of life, that I want a settlement, but for you, dearest daughter. In San Francisco there is an excellent ballet under Boris Volkoff, recently from Moscow, with whom you would realize your

heart's desire, your remarkable potential and happiness, and get away from the sad limitations of your present environment.

"About the enclosed document. You know some of my adventures as a sea captain on the China Coast. Perhaps you don't know the conditions of sinking of the Sarah McDonald. *She was loaded with Chinese immigrants, bound for San Francisco, and although I fought to the utmost to save the vessel, there was considerable loss of life, the memory of which has been a great burden to me since that day. Indeed, there are times when I think I should have gone down with the ship. It is only the thought of you, my lovely, talented daughter, that has buoyed me in those times. In your happiness and fulfillment, I shall find my own.*

"Should I not get a settlement from Van Sickle, I fear I shall not see you again. In which case, you must take the enclosed document to Mr. Wong at the Chinese Freemason Lodge, and he will know what to do. Yr. ever-loving father." Holmes looked up from the document. "There follows his signature," he said, *"Samuel D. O'Shaunessy."*

Holmes folded the letter and restored it to its envelope. I glanced at our young visitor. Her eyes were bright with tears. Then Holmes did one of those spontaneous things which inevitably take me by surprise. Without looking at the maiden, he reached his long fingers into an inner pocket, and produced a folded linen handkerchief which he shook out and extended towards her at arm's length.

She took the fabric, and wiped her eyes. She blew her nose. "Thank you," she said. "That was kind of you." She folded the hanky carefully, and gave it back to Holmes.

He restored it to his pocket without a word, then studied the second document. "This is written in Chinese," he said.

"Yes, it is," was the reply.

"'Inside Buddha sits dignified,'" deciphered Holmes. He looked up. "That is the legend hanging outside the Chinese Freemason Lodge, here in Rossland, is it not?"

"Oh, is it?" replied our visitor "I have never studied Chinese, though my father did, of course."

Holmes looked again at the sheet of aged rice paper. "There is more," he said. "It looks like Tibetan. Indecipherable to me. There are also two signatures here. In Chinese. And that is all." He folded the papers and replaced them in the ancient envelope. "You said that your father was on his way to the Van Sickle mine, Miss O'Shaunessy."

"That's what he told me."

"At this time of night? It is past midnight."

"Business is conducted here at all hours, Mr. Holmes. All manner of business." She paused. "I should be on the dance floor." She arose and adjusted her Spanish shawl. "It is what my dear father says that troubles me, about not seeing me again unless he gets a settlement from Mr. Van Sickle." Her eyes glistened with fresh tears as she adjusted the shawl around her dark hair. "I would be most grateful, Mr. Holmes, if you could look into the matter for me."

Before I could move to assist her, she had opened the door and swept out of the room, leaving Holmes with the ancient Chinese rice paper envelope in his hand.

CHAPTER THREE

The Van Sickle Mine Adventure

Late though it was, Holmes felt the matter was urgent enough to rouse our fellow-traveller, Sir Matthew Begbie.

"Percy Van Sickle!" exclaimed that worthy, pulling on his trowsers. "Good Lord. I thought he was retired long since."

"According to the young lady," said Holmes, "he is back. Drawn, no doubt, by the new strike in the mine that bears his name."

"As I remember it, the Van Sickle property was shared by a number of partners, Van Sickle retaining major ownership."

"What about O'Shaunessy?"

"Right or wrong, O'Shaunessy has no legal claim. I remember the incident plainly. There was no documentation."

"So any argument he has with Van Sickle will have no legal basis."

"None."

"Then I'm afraid there is trouble brewing," said Sherlock Holmes.

In a few minutes, dressed for the outside, we passed through the crowded dining room to seek the advice of the proprietor, Hardrock McKinnon. Late though it was, we found him in his quarters, a sitting room quite elegantly furnished for such a backwoods establishment.

"We must apologize," said Begbie.

Behind the heavy door and sumptuous curtains, the raucous sounds of merry-makers and band music from the dining room was subdued. Books lined the walls. A comfortable divan, flanked by easy chairs, faced a glowing fireplace. Beside the couch, a table held an oil lamp and a silver tray from which crystal glasses and a whisky decanter refracted the lamp-light.

"Gentlemen, you catch me at a busy moment," said the diminutive Hardrock. He gestured to a roll-top desk, at which he had been working. "But do come in. Join me for a night cap."

"We must apologize," said Begbie. "But there appears to be some urgency in a matter which has just materialized."

"Another urgent matter?" Hardrock was pouring liberal amounts of whisky into the crystal tumblers. "There's a shipment of gold going down the Cariboo tomorrow. It's a busy time." He added a splash of soda water and handed out the drinks.

"It's Sam O'Shaunessy," said Begbie. "He's out to get a settlement from Percy Van Sickle, now that Percy has struck it rich."

"Percy? He won't give up a thing! It's twenty years or more since their partnership broke up."

"I remember it," said Begbie. "I always felt it was justice miscarried. Where is Percy now?"

"At the mine, I should think, if he's here at all."

"So late?"

"They'll be working all night getting the shipment ready for tomorrow. There's a coach outside will take you, if you can find the driver. He's likely in the bar. Tell him hullo from me."

Through all this, Holmes and I had remained silent, Holmes less interested in the conversation than in our surroundings and the many artifacts which the place contained, books, Indian relics and the like. In particular, a Chinese dragon with glaring eyes and exposed fangs seemed to catch his interest. Beyond the dragon, on the wall, hung a cloak, an outdoor garment of some dark hue, and below the cloak, half-hidden against the wall, stood a pair of expensive riding boots. There was fresh mud upon them. Holmes' eyes narrowed.

The dining room was still boisterous when we returned, the band playing discordant ragtime to which the girls danced with considerable vigor, if not grace. Adding to the uproar, the tables were now full of miners fresh from the creek, slaking their thirst with whisky and tankards of beer. A moment of enquiry from a group of sober citizens served to identify the coachman, whom we promptly engaged to take us to the Van Sickle mine. But enquire as we might, no one appeared to have seen Van Sickle himself.

The rain had ceased to fall. In the vicinity of the mine, the ground was churned into mud half-way up one's calves, and I was grateful for the heavy boots I wore. A low log building, heavily constructed, stood near the mine entrance. In front of the building a cart, drawn by four great oxen, waited patiently. The cart in turn was attended by a group of armed men, conversing in a monotone, yet with a pervasive air of excitement and anticipation. A senior member of the group recognized Sir Matthew, and came forward to greet him.

"Mulligan!" exclaimed Begbie. "After all these years! Struck it rich, have you?"

"I got a piece of it," replied Mulligan with a grin. "There's a million dollars in gold," he gestured over his shoulder. "Ready to go down the Cariboo first thing in the morning. We'll have a body-guard of twenty men for the transfer."

"Good. Just like old times!" Begbie was enjoying himself. "Is Van Sickle about?"

"I haven't seem 'im."

"Where might he be?"

"He's got a house just down the road. He might be there."

We followed the fellow's directions. The "road," as he called it, was a morass of mud mounded with earth from the diggings, littered with discarded timbers, broken mining equipment and the like. We stumbled along it in the dark, lit fitfully by a pale moon which was now showing itself through the storm clouds.

Presently we came upon a log shack emerging from a sea of mud and bramble bushes. There was no sign of life. We made our way up to the house, and Begbie knocked on the heavy door. There was no response, but under his hand the portal slowly swung open, revealing the dark interior. A taper flared in Holmes' fingers, but it did little to illuminate beyond the entrance. He stepped through the open door, and held up his flickering light.

"Good Lord!" muttered Sherlock Holmes.

Before us, on the grubby floor, near the wall, lay the inert form of Sam O'Shaunessy. Dried blood had caked in his hair and congealed

on the floor-boards beside him. He had been killed by a vicious blow
to the head from a blunt instrument. One bloody hand reached to the
naked plaster of the wall, on which was a single Chinese character.

"Lotus," said Holmes.

At this moment, the taper in Holmes' fingers burned down, so that
he was obliged to let it go. It floated to the floor and went out. As it
did so, there was the creak of a door at the back of the house. A glim-
mer of light appeared, and approached the room where we crouched in
the dark. A moment later the door pushed wider, and a cloaked figure
entered, carrying a dark lantern. I was aware of a sudden movement
beside me, a scuffle and a cry. The lantern fell from the hands of our
nocturnal visitor, and went out. Quickly I struck another vespa, to discover Holmes with a baritsu hold on the invader. The cloak had fallen
back, and revealed the angry, blazing eyes and dark hair of the beautiful Dolores O'Shaunessy.

I picked up the fallen lantern and re-lit it. As I did so, I was aware
of a shift of focus of the lady's eyes. They widened in shock and in
horror, as the light revealed the bloody body of her father.

"Oh, my God," she whispered.

I had never before seen Holmes in such a predicament. He released
his hold on the lady, but she promptly staggered under the emotional
impact of her discovery. So Holmes was obliged to seize her again, to
prevent her from falling to the floor. For a moment, he cradled her in
his arms, attempting to soothe her distress, then as I put down the
lantern, she straightened up, and with immense courage and self-con-
trol, she took the light and went closer to the body. As she knelt beside
it I could feel Holmes divided between compassion for the lady and
concern lest her actions destroy clues that might reveal the miscreant.

A few minutes passed. The lady then rose and turned, quite imperious in her manner. Her eyes flashed in the lamplight. She pointed to
the bloody sign on the wall.

"Do you understand that inscription, Mr. Holmes?"

"It says 'Lotus'," said Holmes.

"I read it as a command from my dear dead father, that justice be
done, Mr. Holmes."

It was with some difficulty that Holmes diverted the young woman
from taking over. Finally we took her into the kitchen and sat her
down, wrapped in her cloak, and Holmes tersely explained to her that

to bring the evil-doer to justice it was necessary to have incontrovertible proof of his identity. Holmes told her that he was prepared to assemble such proof if she would keep out of the way.

There were the remnants of a fire in the kitchen stove, which I stoked up; exploring the sparsely-stocked selves, I was able to come up with a cup of hot tea for her.

I joined Holmes in the other room, where I found him on his knees beside the body of the late Sam O'Shaunessy. Holmes had lit two additional lamps, which stood on the floor beside him, and threw dark shadows across the room. Of Begbie there was no sign.

"Where is Sir Matthew?" I asked.

"He thought it wise to bring in the local authorities," said Holmes. "He has gone off to do so."

I could not at once see what my friend was up to. It was only when I went closer that I saw that in one slender hand he held a crystal whisky glass, which reflected the lamps in a thousand points of light. In his other hand, he had a small camel-hair brush, such as a lady might use on a Sunday afternoon watercolour painting excursion. He was carefully applying a thin layer of white powder on the surface of the whisky glass.

"Fingerprints," he grunted.

And indeed, as Holmes blew away the powder, an unmistakable pattern of lines and whorls of fingerprints emerged under the lamp-light.

"They are the prints of Hardrock McKinnon," said Holmes. "I borrowed the glass from which he had been drinking."

"Good Lord!" I exclaimed.

Holmes carefully laid aside the whisky glass, and, handkerchief in hand, reached into the shadows for an object I had not previously observed. As he brought it into the light, I recognized the cudgel we had last seen in the hands of Sam O'Shaunessy earlier in the day. Its heavy blunt end was now smeared with dried blood and human hair.

"Lead," muttered Holmes.

"What?"

"The blunt end. Hollowed out, and filled with lead. A vicious weapon." Carefully he laid the grim object down beside the body, and taking up the delicate paint brush, he applied the white powder to its slender shaft. In a moment, he blew off the residue as before, and fingerprints appeared. Holmes then put the murder weapon and the crystal goblet side by side, and examined them through his magnifying glass.

"What do you say, Watson?" he grunted.

I peered through the lens. "With no training in the matter," I exclaimed, "I would say the prints are identical. Whoever handled this whisky glass is the same individual that wielded this terrible weapon."

"Hardrock McKinnon," said Holmes.

At this juncture, there was the sound of horses outside. The front door opened and Sir Matthew entered, followed by two N.W.M.P. constables of tender age.

"Murder has been done, gentlemen," said Sherlock Holmes. "The guilty party is Hardrock McKinnon, proprietor of the Rossland Hotel. He must be taken into custody."

The young constables looked askance at the scene, the lamps on the floor casting long shadows, the bony form of Sherlock Holmes standing over the body of Sam O'Shaunessy, its bloody hand reaching towards the cryptic message on the wall. In the doorway to the kitchen, stood the lady Dolores, her black Spanish shawl obscuring all but her dark eyes.

"What, sir, may I ask, is your proof of Mr. McKinnon's guilt in this matter?"

"Fingerprints," replied Holmes tersely.

The young officer turned to Sir Matthew, who nodded to him in a reassuring manner. "Do as Mr. Holmes says," said Sir Matthew. "There will be plenty of time for enquiry after the man is arrested."

At these quiet words the policemen sprang to attention, saluted, and moved swiftly to the door. A moment later there was a sound of horses' hooves as they departed on their mission. With their going, an older policeman had entered, grizzled of beard and mustache, taking in the scene with an experienced eye. Evidently an old acquaintance of Sir Matthew, he exchanged a few quiet words with him, lighting a battered briar pipe.

"I'll stay and keep an eye on things," I heard him say.

Holmes had turned his attention to wrapping up his exhibits — the crystal goblet, and the bloodstained cudgel — in such a manner as to protect their crucial fingerprint evidence. He put the articles into the care of the senior officer.

Dolores O'Shaunessy moved into the room, and the lamps on the floor multiplied her elongated shadow.

"What now, Mr. Holmes?" she asked.

"There is little more one can do here," replied Holmes.

The young lady crossed to the body of her father, and stood for a moment in silence.

"I think we must now seek out your Mr. Wong," said Sherlock Holmes.

CHAPTER FOUR

The Smiling Buddha

The sky was paling in the east as we again found ourselves in Sourdough Alley. From the makeshift roofs, protruding stove-pipes and jerry-built chimneys were beginning to smoke, heralding a new day.

At the Chinese Cultural Centre the door was already open, and as we approached we heard the deep, sonorous vibration of a struck gong. Inside the building, a ritual was being conducted. The gong was struck again, and a group of perhaps eight or ten modestly clothed Orientals rose from their knees, where they had presumably been in prayer. They bowed and smiled at us as they made their way out into the approaching day.

An elderly Chinese gentleman who had apparently been conducting the "service" — it was he who had struck the gong — now stood alone in front of us, a smile on his face, a look of enquiry in his raised eyebrows. He clasped his hands in front of him and bowed to us. Behind him, dominating the modest room, was a Buddha of benign aspect. It was of considerable age, it seemed to my uninformed eye.

The image was encrusted with ancient gold leaf, its head slightly inclined, lips parted in a smile. Between its two clasped hands, carved and gilded, dulled by the passage of years, was a lotus blossom, held as if in offering.

Holmes produced Sam O'Shaunessy's document. "Mr. Wong?" he enquired.

"Yes," replied the old gentleman.

"This paper belongs to the young lady. It may interest you."

Dolores took the ancient rice paper envelope from Holmes' hand. "This was given me by my father, Captain Sam O'Shaunessy, who was in command of the steamship *Sarah McDonald* when she sunk in a storm many years ago."

Wong's mouth turned down in a tragic expression of grief. "Yes," he said. "I was there."

Holmes' eyes sharpened. "You remember?" he said.

"We were bringing a shipload of immigrants, and the golden Buddha, from Shanghai," said the old man. "The Buddha was from Tibet. It was saved with many Chinese lives when the ship was wrecked. The Chinese community here is deeply indebted to Captain Sam for saving those lives, and mine, in peril of his own."

"I am most pleased to hear that," said the lady, in fervent tones. Involuntarily, she clasped the ancient Celestial's hands in her own. Their eyes met in silent communication.

After a moment, Wong spoke softly. "I would be privileged to read the letter," he said.

Dolores handed the rice paper envelope to the old man. He took it in his gnarled work-worn fingers, opened it, and took out the card.

"Inside Buddha sits dignified," said Wong.

"Yes?" said Holmes. "And the other?"

"It is a koan. In Tibetan Sanskrit. *'Behold the jewel in the heart of the lotus.'"*

"Is that not a phrase recited in praise of Buddha?" queried Holmes. His voice was sharp.

"Yes. In Tibet, using the prayer-wheel. Each turn of the wheel is a prayer."

"What is its significance here?"

The old man shook his head. He looked tired. "I am sorry to say that I do not know," he said. "It is a prayer. That is all." He handed the document back to Dolores, with an apologetic shrug of his thin shoulders.

With this action, Holmes' attention shifted. He was gazing intently at the Buddha, which smiled benignly in the rays of the early morning sun. Holmes' eyes went from the open mouth to the clasped hands. Abruptly he moved, his magnifying glass to his eye. The object of his interest was the golden lotus clasped in the carved hands of the image.

"What is this?" he cried, his voice sounding harsh in the subdued atmosphere of the Buddhist temple. Wong turned to him with a start.

"Is it not the formal carving of a lotus blossom?" cried Holmes.

The old man followed Holmes' intent gaze. "That floral decoration is so familiar to me that I had not thought of it as a lotus," he said in gentle tones.

With inquisitive fingers, Holmes was feeling the ancient, gold-encrusted surface. After a moment, he sat back on his heels.

"The heart of the lotus," he said, then, "'Inside the Buddha sits dignified.'"

Holmes rose to his feet. "'Inside the Buddha,'" he repeated, and in one direct motion stretched out his slender hand towards the open mouth. For a moment he felt about inside. There was a click, and to my amazement the lotus blossom opened up its carved surface to reveal within it a great jewel, which glowed in the rays of the rising sun.

There is little more to tell. Hardrock McKinnon was arrested for the murder of Sam O'Shaunessy, whose funeral was attended by miners and escorts of the wagon train preparing to ship a million dollars in gold down the Cariboo Road.

The beautiful Dolores O'Shaunessy shared our coach on the return to Vancouver. On the road, we passed the great ox-cart, laden with its valuable cargo, escorted by twenty stalwart men. Recognizing her and the much-honoured Sir Matthew Begbie, the stout fellows raised a cheer as we swept by them on the narrow trail.

Through Begbie's efforts it was later disclosed that the young lady's father, Sam O'Shaunessy, had indeed been registered as part owner of the Van Sickle mine, and the issue had been deliberately obscured by the rascally Hardrock McKinnon to his own advantage.

In addition to the magnificent ruby — "the jewel in the heart of the lotus" — the lovely Dolores was subsequently awarded a most substantial amount of the proceeds of the Van Sickle mine, with which she built a music hall in San Francisco. There she appeared as prima ballerina under the direction of the Russian impresario, Boris Volkoff, until the hall burned down in the earthquake of 1905.

Holmes and I never did catch up with Percy Van Sickle, who, after all, seemed to be as much a victim of circumstance as Sam O'Shaunessy.

Back in Vancouver, Holmes took the opportunity of the coincidental visit of Asahel Curtis, the gifted photographer who was to record so much of the Yukon Gold Rush for posterity, to query the optical values of a camera lens capable of getting extremely close to its subject.

"What sort of subjects do you have in mind?" asked Mr. Curtis.

"Fingerprints," said Sherlock Holmes.